SIZZ

"Damn you, Gregory Ferris!"

Dismay, fury and frustration clashed within Stacy. "What do you want from me?"

Greg stood and looked across the room at her. A long moment passed before he spoke. "I want this marriage business between us finished."

Stacy was confused by his words. "But I told you I'd get a divorce."

Shaking his head, Greg put on his cowboy hat and started from the kitchen. "Not that way. I want it to end the way it began. I won't contest the divorce...."

He turned in the doorway to gaze at her, and Stacy felt an ominous foreboding. "If?" she asked.

"Not if. When. When you sleep with me again."

Dear Reader,

I think all writers look to their past when writing. I
have wonderful memories of vacations spent in
Colorado, of riding my best friend's horse and of
seeing those great Westerns on television. You know,
the ones in which the hero always wore a white hat
and was incredibly handsome and brave and honest
and good.

Now that I'm lucky enough to live here, I still find
Colorado a beautiful, magical place. Although I
don't live in the San Luis Valley, like the sandhill
cranes I'm regularly drawn to the area, and I knew I
had to set a story there.

Over the years, my children have dragged home
abandoned or abused animals—dogs, cats, rabbits
and even a rat—so the idea of Greg dragging home
an abused horse came naturally. I also feel that too
often in stories a know-nothing city gal comes in and
swipes the hero from under the noses of all the
country gals. And that's why I decided Stacy was
going to keep her man.

Nothing is more fun for a writer than all the
elements of a story coming together. I hope you
enjoy reading about Stacy and Greg as much as I
enjoyed writing about them.

Sincerely,

Jeanne Allan

THE COWBOY
NEXT DOOR
Jeanne Allan

Harlequin Books

TORONTO • NEW YORK • LONDON
AMSTERDAM • PARIS • SYDNEY • HAMBURG
STOCKHOLM • ATHENS • TOKYO • MILAN
MADRID • WARSAW • BUDAPEST • AUCKLAND

For Bette and Bill, who have shared
fifty golden years of love and romance.
Wishing you many more.

Original hardcover edition published as
ECHOES OF LOVE
in 1993 by Mills & Boon Limited

ISBN 0-373-03286-2

Harlequin Romance first edition October 1993

THE COWBOY NEXT DOOR

CHAPTER ONE

THE pink and white dress was either an easterner's vision of "the Old West" or the creation of a cake decorator gone mad. Broderie anglaise cascaded from the neck and sleeves while miles of ruffles circled the full skirt and white bows sprouted with drunken abandon. Stacy Hamelton loathed the dress.

The couple spun by again. The woman must be the new schoolteacher whom Stacy's mother had repeatedly mentioned just a shade too casually over the past two months. One hundred years ago a teacher in Colorado wouldn't have dared show her face, much less her legs, on a dance floor. Not that the legs exposed by the flaring skirt were so great. For one thing, they were short. The teacher was attractive enough, with her reddish-gold curls bouncing in time with the music. Most men would undoubtedly call her pretty, but the woman reminded Stacy of a faithful beagle who'd followed her around years ago with that same sappy look of adoration on his face.

The object of the woman's adoration didn't seem to mind. On the contrary, the look on Gregory Ferris's face made it nauseatingly clear that he approved of his partner. Someone ought to tell him that in a few years the woman would probably run to fat.

Whoever told him, it wouldn't be Stacy Hamelton. She was thrilled that Greg was otherwise occupied. It gave her time to rehearse what she wanted to say to him. Rehearse. At one time she would have laughed at the notion that she needed to choose her words carefully around Greg. That was a lifetime ago. Butterflies invaded her stomach. Last week her idea to approach Greg tonight had seemed the perfect plan. Surrounded by friends and neighbors, their encounter would be brisk and impersonal. She'd politely recite her request; he'd politely agree. Now, seeing him, Stacy wished she'd stuck to her original plan to write him a letter. So what if he thought she was a coward? Greg's opinions meant nothing to her. Besides, she wasn't afraid of him. If her knees were practically knocking together, well, naturally she was a little nervous. It had been a long time... A long time, she reiterated to herself. She was a big girl now. Much too old to be reduced to a mass of quivering jelly by gray eyes warm with amusement. Not that Greg would be amused to see her.

"That's Lucy Fraser, a new teacher at the school, dancing with Greg," Lloyd Hamelton said at Stacy's side. "She's a cozy little armful."

Stacy glanced at her father. "I didn't realize you were such an authority."

"I may be your father, but I'm still a man. And I'd say Greg agrees with me." He squeezed her arm. "Want me to beat him up for playing fast and loose with my baby?"

"Don't be silly. I couldn't care less what Greg does."

Her father snorted. "Since when? You know damn well ever since you were a kid you planned to marry Greg."

"I was a kid. Now I'm twenty-four and I've discarded such silly ideas along with my toys." The music stopped and Greg and his partner disappeared into the crowd across the room. Stacy relaxed. He hadn't seen her. "And you know damn well," she mimicked her father's tone, "it's time you did."

"Stacy Hamelton," her father said in mock censure. "Ladies don't swear. Your mama would wash your mouth out with soap."

Stacy looked across the room. Ruth Hamelton had been sending her daughter looks of mingled sympathy and reproach for the past half hour. "She has other things on her mind."

Her father followed her gaze. "She's never liked you leaving the Valley. Her heart's set on you marrying Greg."

"Then she'll have to un-set it. Greg's no more interested in me than I am in him."

Her father eyed Stacy's trim figure clothed in a severely cut red silk dress. "Maybe you ought to dress more like Lucy Fraser. More feminine."

"Are you serious?" In her father's book, women were supposed to be cute and dependent and slightly addlebrained. Never mind that his own wife was bright and competent. According to her mother, the trick was not to let a man know you were as capable as he was. Stacy refused to play such games. "I'd look like a decorated Maypole in that pink number she's wearing. Lucy Fraser might be cute, but I'm just——" she thought of her five feet eight inches "—tall."

"You always let Greg think of you as his little brother."

"Ten years ago you thought it was more important for me to learn how to rope a calf than to sew a fancy dress," Stacy pointed out.

"Ten years ago I assumed you'd marry Greg and settle down to be a rancher's wife. Roping cattle seemed a necessary skill."

"That's what you get for assuming," Stacy said. "I don't have occasion to rope many cows at the bank."

"The bank," her father echoed in disgust. "Don't you think it's time you gave up that foolishness and came back here where you belong?"

"Maybe she doesn't belong here any more."

Stacy's heart lurched at the slow, familiar drawl and she stiffened as an arm slipped around her waist. "I don't." She summoned the courage to meet cool gray eyes. He didn't need to know that she was quaking inside.

"Slumming, Slim?"

No one else ever called her that. Her sudden breathlessness was nothing more than learned behavior and habit, a meaningless residue from adolescence that would disappear with time. "Don't call me Slim," she said, her voice sharp with annoyance.

Greg Ferris gave her a mocking look. "Here to show us backward country cousins how a real city slicker looks?"

Mockery was easier to deal with than—than the other. "It's always amusing to remind myself how the other half lives." She refused to gratify him by making an issue of his arm.

"She looks like an adolescent boy," Lloyd grumbled.

"You spent too much of your youth on bucking broncs, Lloyd. Your brains are scrambled." Greg's slow inspection of Stacy was more insult than approval. "Your little girl looks damned sexy. That new outrageously short cut makes her hair look blacker, shows off her high cheekbones and makes her look mighty independent. She looks as if she doesn't give a damn what anyone thinks about her. Some men view that as quite a challenge," he added in a low drawl, his arm tightening around her waist.

Hot anger sliced through Stacy's body. Greg was deliberately trying to provoke her. Pretending his constricting embrace threw her off balance, she flailed her arms, in the process whacking Greg solidly in his midsection with her elbow. "I'm sorry," she cooed. "You were saying something about men finding me a challenge?" She blatantly fluttered her eyelashes. "Does that include present company?"

The lines at the corners of Greg's eyes deepened. "Accepting that kind of challenge is kids' stuff." Satisfaction glinted briefly in his eyes as he saw his remark hit target.

"Well, Greg——" totally oblivious to his daughter's smoldering anger, Lloyd Hamelton slapped the younger man's back "—since this shindig is celebrating the fact that Mary Beth has finally taken Tom out of circulation, that leaves you about the most eligible bachelor in the San Luis Valley." Winking at Stacy, her father barged ahead. "When are you taking the plunge? Maybe you can talk this daughter of mine into coming home."

"Dad!" Marriage was the last thing she wanted to discuss in Greg's presence. "I'm perfectly happy with my life as it is."

"I'm getting to be an old man. I want to see my grandchildren before I die."

Stacy scowled fiercely at her father. "Keep it up and I'll murder you myself. You're too ornery to die any other way."

"Look at old Charlie. His arthritis is so bad he can't pick up a newspaper, much less a grandson," Lloyd said plaintively.

"Charlie doesn't have a grandson." She refused to look at Greg, but she was very aware of him beside her.

"Neither do I," Lloyd said unrepentantly. "And if I have to wait around for you, I probably never will."

"You didn't give your father a grandchild until you were thirty-five," Stacy argued uselessly.

"And look what I got stuck with," Lloyd said. "A mouthy bean pole who thinks she's too good to live on a ranch. No son of mine would have run away to the city." He gave Greg a dark look. "Not that anyone around here did anything to stop her."

"Now, Lloyd," Greg said, his slow drawl more pronounced than usual, "you know Slim was just a kid when she left."

"She looks pretty damned grown-up to me now."

"Cutting her hair doesn't mean she's a grown woman."

Stacy felt her cheeks flame at Greg's disparaging comment. Lifting her chin a defiant notch, she deliberately misunderstood him. "Greg's afraid I'm not through growing taller. He wouldn't want a bean-pole wife towering over him."

"You know how lazy I am, Slim." His smile failed to warm his eyes. "Maybe I'm just waiting until you get tall enough that I don't have to bend over to kiss you."

Stacy's heart leaped like a startled pronghorn. "You'll have a long wait, because I don't intend to grow one more inch."

"Have you ever noticed how seldom life turns out as you intend?" Greg's gaze was politely interested.

"Well, it sure hasn't turned out as I intended," Stacy's father said in disgust, "and I'm getting sick of Jake bragging that he's getting rid of the last of six girls and Mary Beth only twenty. I told him Stacy'd get hitched when she was good and ready and not a minute before." He fixed an aggrieved eye on her. "It might've shut him up, but don't think it'll shut me up." He waved toward the dance floor. "Take her away and dance with her, Greg." Stacy's father walked away muttering.

"I don't want to dance with you," Stacy said.

"Tough." Greg pulled her on to the dance floor. "I wouldn't want Lloyd to haul out his shotgun. Mary Beth might not appreciate blood on the floor at her wedding dance."

"Mary Beth wouldn't notice. She can't see anything but Tom. She thinks he's a Greek god, movie star and western hero straight out of a Louis L'Amour novel all wrapped up in one." Greg's right arm burned her waist and his left hand imprisoned her right. If it wouldn't create the very gossip she hoped to avoid, she'd have it out with Greg right here on the dance floor.

"That's the way a wife should see her husband." Sliding his right hand lower, he pulled her closer.

Stacy felt like grinding her teeth. Preferably with Greg's head between them. He was taking advantage of her forced compliancy to infuriate her. "I should have known you'd want a wife who saw you through such rosy-colored glasses that she didn't bother to dig into the real you."

"There's lots you should know, Slim, but I doubt you do."

The scent of his after-shave was one that haunted her sleepless nights. "I know I don't want you as a husband." Across the room her father was watching them complacently. "One of these days Dad's going to push me too far and I'll tell him. It would be worth it to see the look on his face."

"Would it?"

Stacy looked up into expressionless gray eyes. "Don't get yourself in a lather over it," she said in a mocking voice. Greg seldom bothered to get himself in a lather over anything.

"C.B. always said there was no point in looking for trouble," Greg said. "It will find you soon enough. No doubt he was thinking of you when he said it."

"More likely you." She followed Greg's steps as a female vocalist wailed of lost love and broken hearts. "He may have been your uncle, but he wasn't totally blind."

Greg was silent. The melancholy music was interlaced with the sounds of people talking and laughing, dishes clattering and chairs scraping the wooden floor. Mary Beth had gone overboard with flowers. Saffron-colored daisies, golden chrysanthemums and yellow carnations filled a multitude of white containers and a heavy, floral aroma hung oppressively in the air. Stacy's stomach contracted. It was her own fault for stupidly attending the wedding. She should have known better. Writing him a letter would have served her purpose and been much smarter. And less painful. The imprint of Greg's hand branded her hip. His body heat scorched her skin. Unshed tears swelled her throat. If only one could erase the past. She swallowed hard. She couldn't erase the past, but she had to deal with it.

"We were the original odd trio," Greg said unexpectedly. "A crusty old rancher, a city boy who didn't know one end of a horse from another and the biggest tomboy in the valley."

"You were green as grass."

"And you decided it was your mission to whip me into shape."

"After you took on that bully for me, I owed you."

"A person never realizes how one tiny decision will affect the rest of his life." Greg tightened his grip on her right hand. "Given foresight, I'd have let him steal your lunch."

"I didn't ask for your help," Stacy quickly said.

"Not then."

Stacy stumbled. In a flash three years of hard-won forgetfulness evaporated and she was back at C.B.'s corral, stiff and awkward, stumbling through the explanation, expecting Greg to come to her rescue. "Believe me, I've never regretted anything so much in my entire life as coming to you."

"I believe you, Slim." He paused. "It's long past time we did something about it."

His words turned her to stone. She could no more move her feet than she could work her tongue. Her gaze flew to Greg's face. His eyes were shuttered. The chin was familiarly resolute but the hard mouth belonged to a stranger. There was not the slightest hint of regret or remorse. The sudden sharp catch in her chest was as surprising as it was painful. After all, this was the reason she'd come home this weekend. The reason she'd subjected herself to a wedding after three years of avoiding them. The reason she'd planned this encounter with Greg—to force him into resolving their situation. C.B. had been dead five months. There was no longer any reason to wait. Stacy took a deep breath. "I guess Mother was right. She warned…that is," her voice sounded odd, "she said everyone is counting the days until you announce your engagement to the new schoolteacher."

They were standing near a doorway and Greg pushed her through it into an empty hallway. "Lucy Fraser?" The door swung shut, cutting them off from the crowd and dimming the music.

"Is there more than one?" Stacy backed up against the unyielding hallway wall. "Don't you think she's a little on the fluffy side to be a rancher's wife?"

"Jealous, Slim?" Leaning against the opposite wall, Greg crossed his long legs at the ankle. Two wine-colored patches stained the area above his head.

"Don't be ridiculous. I was merely making conversation. It's no skin off my nose whom you wine and dine." An unseen artist had outlined the stains to resemble a fractured heart. An arrow pierced its center. "When can I wish you and the lucky bride happiness?"

"For someone who's made it crystal-clear I'm not the answer to a maiden's prayer, you're mighty quick to assume someone else would have me."

"I saw the sappy look on that teacher's face while you two were dancing. Just because I can't think of one good reason why any sane, sensible woman would want to marry you——"

"Can't you? You, of all people," anger flashed across his face, momentarily disturbing his calm mask, "ought to be able to come up with at least one."

Stacy sucked in her breath at the painful jab before attempting retaliation. "On second thoughts, I can think of three. Land, money and cows. I'm sure any gold digger would overlook your obvious flaws."

Greg laughed. "Meaning my nose?"

Stacy glared at him, furious her ineffectual insult had amused him instead of angering him. It was another in a long line of occasions when Greg had refused to take her seriously. Not that she cared any longer. "Breaking your nose improved your face. Too bad you didn't break your head while you were at it."

"I rather think that's what the horse had in mind."

"Horse?" She made a derisive face. "The oldest, slowest and stupidest nag on C.B.'s ranch. It's a wonder we didn't all laugh ourselves to death."

"Instead of rushing to my rescue?"

"I was a child," Stacy snapped. "Too softhearted for my own good. Back then I wouldn't even step on a worm on the road after a rainstorm."

"But you do now?" His voice was bored.

"Of course," she lied.

"If you don't consider my crooked nose a drawback in the pursuit of a suitable wife, what is?" His eyes half closed, he appeared on the brink of falling asleep.

"I really haven't given the subject any thought."

"Not planning to be a suitable wife yourself, you mean."

Stacy repressed an urge to kick his legs out from under him. It would be easier to dislodge the San Juan Mountains than to dump Greg on his complacent rear end. Even relaxed, he had the balance of a barn cat and the stability of Blanca Peak. She settled for words. "You're rude, tactless, hard, inflexible and about as warm and cozy as a granite rock. One look at that outfit your schoolteacher is wearing should tell you she has silly, romantic fantasies about ranch life. And you don't have a romantic bone in your body. You're too practical, you expect a woman to saddle her own horse and bait her own fishing hook. When you take a woman outside to look at the moon, you look at the moon. You're a dull country boy who doesn't have an ounce of excitement or romance about him. Besides, you snore."

"Leaving aside the fact that I'm a granite rock," Greg pushed away from the wall and ambled toward her, "I find it difficult to believe that a high school champion barrel racer——" his left hand rested on the wall beside her "—wants a man to saddle her horse or bait her hook. Are you telling me this glossy city finish of yours——" he traced the line of her fringe across her forehead "—goes all the way through?"

"We're not talking about me." Stacy tried to edge away but his body effectively penned her in. She stared at the buttons on his shirt. "We're talking about your intended bride."

"Are we?"

The strange note in Greg's voice brought her head up. The feeble light in the hallway lent his gray eyes the dark, brooding aura of the sky before a storm. His after-shave hinted of musk. The air around them sizzled with a strange tension. "Women like her expect passion, excitement, a sense of adventure." Stacy fought to keep her voice steady. "Sweeping a woman off her feet takes more energy than you're interested in expending."

"You think I'm too lazy to pursue the woman of my dreams?"

Even his voice was slow and lazy. Disquiet prickled over her skin, but she forged ahead. "You'd be perfect for an old-time sultan who expected his harem ladies to come to him."

"I wonder if harem ladies had earlobes as provocative as yours?" He traced the outer edges of her ear.

Stacy swatted at his hand. "Stop that. We're not discussing my ears."

"Maybe you're not, but I am. They've been peeking out from beneath that new hairdo and tantalizing me all evening." He caught a lobe between his thumb and forefinger, his grip tightening when Stacy tried to pull away.

She froze. The cold November air seemed to have invaded the hallway and settled in her spine. "Let go of me." The pressure eased but Greg didn't relinquish his grasp of the tender lobe.

"Do all the men in your life jump to do your bidding? You didn't even say please."

"What do you want, Greg?" A tall artificial tree shared the hallway with them, filtering the overhead light and drawing mottled shadows on Greg's face. "Why are you holding me prisoner in this hallway?"

Greg released her ear to run his fingers through her hair. "You're not a prisoner. We're merely having a discussion about my inability to wax romantic and sweep a woman off her feet."

"We're not having a discussion," Stacy said flatly. "You've got something on your mind, so why don't you say it? If you're trying to frighten me so I'll give you what you want, don't waste your time. You couldn't want it any more than I do."

"Is that so? Is that what this conversation is all about, Slim? Wedding bells in your future?" Greg laced his fingers together at the nape of Stacy's neck. "Someone been sweeping you off your feet?"

"No." Her spine tingled with a vague apprehension. Greg stared down at her, his gray eyes dark and unfathomable. Stacy clutched at his arms to hold him at bay as the strange tension swirled around them. This was only Greg. Easygoing, impossible-to-rile Greg. His muscles moved beneath her palms and she could feel little nubs in the fabric of his jacket.

"Why not?" Greg trailed his thumbs behind Stacy's ears.

"You know why not." She swayed, brushing an arm against some leaves from the artificial tree. Her skin seemed extraordinarily sensitive and through the thin silk of her dress sleeve she imagined she felt every vein in every leaf. "Besides, I'm too tall to be swept off—anywhere."

"I don't think you're too tall." Greg lowered his head. "Let's see, shall we, Slim?"

"No." Reason told her to flee but it was too late. Greg's breath was warm against her lips before he fitted his mouth to hers. He sucked gently on her bottom lip until it caught fire and throbbed with flame. She parted her lips to protest—a protest Greg ignored as he slipped his tongue into her mouth. He tasted of toasts to the bridal couple. The faint music behind them faded totally away to be replaced by the harsh sounds of their breathing. Greg kissed her slowly and intimately.

She tightened her hold on his arms as she sagged against him, unexpected pleasure spiraling through her body, her heart thudding against Greg's chest. From deep within her came a compelling urge to press closer to his inviting warmth. Greg slid his hands from her shoulders and down her back, large, warm hands that cradled her hips and held her firmly against him. Her breasts felt heavy and she burrowed into his body.

Greg drew back, parting their lips with his fingers. "I wasn't quite anticipating that." He ran his calloused thumb lightly over the throbbing surface of Stacy's bottom lip.

The hint of amusement in Greg's voice cut sharply through Stacy's lingering confusion. She snatched back hands that were still entwined in brown hair, at the same time biting down hard on his thumb.

"Ouch! Why the hell did you do that?" He sucked on the tip of his thumb.

"Call it a wedding present for the future Mrs. Greg Ferris. I hope the name means more to her than it ever meant to me."

"It will mean more to any woman on earth than it ever meant to you," he bit out.

Here was the reason for Greg's odd behavior. "I suppose that's why you forced your kiss on me. As punishment."

"I didn't exactly have to use force."

His slow grin roiled her insides. "I was taken by surprise, that's all. I don't like your kisses now any better than I did three years ago when you . . ." Her voice died away under his icy glare.

There was no trace of grin on Greg's face now. "When I what?" he asked in a harsh voice. "Stole your innocence?"

"You didn't exactly steal it." Heat crawled up her face and she stared over her shoulder. "After three years I hardly remember it. Except it was messy and embarrassing and a lot of fuss about nothing."

"Thanks a lot," Greg said in a low, bitter voice.

A pang of guilt knifed through Stacy before she realised that it was exactly what Greg wanted. "Come off it, Greg. Don't expect me to believe your ego is the least bit dented because my first experience with a man didn't exactly move the earth."

"A man doesn't like to hear he was a total flop."

"What would you expect? You'd had too much to drink, and I was totally ignorant."

"Just a couple of dudes." Greg gave a snort of disgust. "Acting like two animals out behind the barn."

"We weren't behind the barn," she said quickly. "We went to that——"

"Sleazy motel in Alamosa. How could I forget? The two of us sneaking in. Tattered curtains that didn't quite meet in the middle so that you were paranoid someone was watching us. And those damned neon lights across the street.'' He cupped her chin in a work-roughened hand and stared pensively at her. "No wonder you remember it as the night from hell.''

This was the first time Greg had ever voiced anything that might be construed as contrition. Nothing in his face gave her a clue to his thoughts. "I try not to remember it at all.'' His grip tightened infinitesimally and then her chin was free.

"Apparently I don't have your remarkable ability to forget the single most frustrating experience of my life,'' Greg said.

Her skin retained the imprint of his hand. "It was a long time ago,'' Stacy said. Greg had wounded her, deeply, painfully. Not a physical wounding, but an agonizing shredding of her heart. In time, her heart had healed, but the healing process had left behind a legacy of bitterness and anger which had festered and grown. She'd come home this weekend determined to confront Greg and settle their situation once and for all. But nothing would be settled if she continued to cling to useless emotions. Greg had opened his heart to another woman. She, too, had to move on. And part of that moving on was to forgive Greg as well as herself. Greg started back to the dance. Stacy caught up to him and touched his arm. "It was a long time ago,'' she repeated. "Something that happened to two other people in some other life. It's time we forgot about it and moved on with our lives. I can't lie and tell you what we did that night will ever be a favorite memory,'' she attempted awkward absolution, "but it has nothing to do with how either of us will be with new partners. When a man and a woman are in love... These things work out.''

"You're speaking from experience, I presume.''

She snatched back her hand at Greg's cool response. "That's none of your business. I was merely trying to——"

"Patronize me?" Greg turned a stony countenance to her. "Since when did you give a damn about my feelings?"

"I merely thought after three years of crucifying each other it was time we grew up and consigned the episode to where it belongs."

"In the attic with all our other outgrown toys, I suppose." Brushing aside the edges of his unbuttoned jacket, he slid his hands into his pant pockets.

"Exactly. Surely after all this time we can be adult about it. We made a mistake but now it's time to forget it and move forward with our lives. You want——"

"To be free," he interjected. "These past few years I've felt as trapped as a cow caught in a mess of barbed wire."

The fierce remark threw Stacy off balance. "I'm sorry. I didn't——"

He ignored her flustered apology. "I've never shared your aversion to marriage. In spite of my parents' divorce, I'm all for the institution." His voice was impersonal; his gaze brushed past her as he stared down the hall. "I'm thirty years old. A man starts thinking about his future. About his children."

His last word stunned her. "Children?" Unexpected pain jabbed behind her eyeballs.

"Your dad wants grandchildren. I want children." His voice changed subtly. "You didn't think this situation could go on forever, did you?"

"No. Of course not." Greg's children would be brown-haired, gray-eyed miniatures of him. The boys would inherit the Ferris swagger, that slow-moving, rolling gait that spoke confidently to the world. Once she'd thought Greg's children would be her...

Stacy forcefully reminded herself that Greg's future children were of no interest to her. "I'm more eager than you to put this all behind me. To end it once and for all." Moisture stung her eyes.

Greg peered intently down at her face. "Tears, from you? I haven't seen you cry since that day——"

"This doesn't mean what you think. I'm happy, that's all. Ecstatically happy. Besides," Stacy brushed a shaky finger across her cheeks, "women are supposed to cry at weddings."

"Will you cry at mine?" Greg asked whimsically.

Light fell on a hank of brown hair that had strayed down over Greg's brow and Stacy fought a strong urge to brush back the silken threads. "Don't I always?"

It was just Stacy's luck that the last person on earth she wanted to encounter was standing in the ladies' room combing her hair. Stacy wet a paper towel with cold water and patted her eyes. Not that there were any traces left of her stupid tears. She hated the fact that she'd cried in front of Greg. Especially when she was deliriously happy that they'd finally agreed to settle things. She ignored the woman who was surreptitiously studying her.

"I don't believe we've met. I'm Lucy Fraser," the petite strawberry blonde said. "I moved here this summer to teach in the elementary school."

Stacy met the other woman's eyes in the mirror. "Stacy Hamelton," she introduced herself.

"I know. When I saw Greg Ferris leave the dance with you, I asked who you were. I guess you're back for a visit." A slight rising inflexion turned the statement into a question.

"Yes." Stacy was in no mood for an inquisition.

"I understand you and Greg have been friends for a long time." Lucy played with a tube of lipstick, her gaze on Stacy.

"We've known each other a long time," Stacy agreed.

The teacher stared dubiously at Stacy in the mirror. "That's not quite the same thing."

Stacy dragged a comb through her hair, welcoming the pain when she encountered a tangle. "I'm not in love with him, if that's what you're asking."

A bright flush covered the woman's face but she didn't drop her gaze. "It's how Greg feels that matters."

"He doesn't love me either," Stacy said. "You needn't worry." Part of her was proud of the lack of emotion in her voice; another part of her was stunned at her involvement in such an extraordinary conversation with a complete stranger. The meeting with Greg had shaken her more than she'd anticipated.

"I wasn't exactly worried. Not that Greg isn't worth worrying about." More confident now, Lucy flashed an enormous smile. "I adore western men. There's something about them."

"Men are men," Stacy said in a neutral voice. She had no desire to pursue this conversation.

Oblivious to any lack of interest in her audience, Lucy said, "No, they're not. Western men even walk differently from eastern men. They sort of amble and swagger and ooze masculinity. Maybe it's the way their tight jeans show off their long legs and hug their nice bottoms."

Instantly a picture of Greg sauntering across the corral was etched on Stacy's mind. "I hadn't noticed." She gripped her comb tightly, her fingernails digging painfully into her palm.

"How can you miss it? All this rampant masculinity. I feel like a kid turned loose in a candy store." Lucy smoothed down her dress. "There's something so sexy about a cowboy. The boys I met at college were children compared to men like Greg."

This was the woman Greg wanted, this piece of frivolous nonsense? Stacy carefully placed her comb in her purse. "We're talking about Gregory Ferris, not a John Wayne movie."

"I know that. It's just that Greg's so physically fit with those wide shoulders, narrow hips and flat stomach. That hunk of brown hair always hanging down just begs a woman to brush it back into place." Lucy looked dreamily into the mirror above the sink. "I feel so delicate beside Greg. He's so lean and tall."

"He's only three inches over six feet when he's in his stockinged feet," Stacy snapped.

Lucy smiled as she fluffed her curls. "I'm amazed that Greg managed to remain single all these years. What's the matter with the women around here? Are you blind or stupid?"

Stacy closed her purse with a loud, decisive snap. "Greg isn't single."

"Of course he is." Lucy swung away from the mirror, her face bewildered. "I thought..." Her voice died away as she stared at Stacy. "You?" she asked in a strangled voice.

Stacy bestowed a condescending smile on the other woman. "For the past three years Greg Ferris and I have been husband and wife."

CHAPTER TWO

"Once again your mouth outran your brain," Stacy told her twin in the mirror as she creamed her face. "No wonder your father calls you a mouthy bean pole." Just because she'd taken an instant, unreasonable dislike to Lucy Fraser. It wasn't the schoolteacher's fault that she was from Detroit and thought that all cowboys did was stride around in tight jeans. The silly woman probably thought they still serenaded cows from horseback. Woe betide Lucy when she discovered Greg couldn't carry a tune if he had a suitcase. All of which was beside the point. Stacy had no business telling Greg's sweetheart that he was married to Stacy. A fact Stacy knew full well the minute the damning words had tripped from her lips. Once spoken, there was no use denying the statement. She could hardly laugh and claim she was joking. Scrambling to recover, Stacy had stitched together a patchwork explanation of lies and half-truths, for which Lucy Fraser had fallen hook, line and sinker. A bittersweet thought curved Stacy's lips. C.B. would have been tickled pink to hear he was the villain in the piece.

Explaining why Stacy divulged a secret marriage to a comparative stranger had been tricky, but Stacy had gone confidingly woman-to-woman on that point, convincing Lucy that she had spoken from the most altruistic of motives. A brilliant move, Stacy congratulated herself in the mirror. Lucy Fraser would keep Stacy's secret. Any woman who was so smitten by Gregory Ferris that she practically drooled when she talked about him would never do anything that might hurt "sexy, oozing with masculinity" Greg.

Standing up, Stacy walked to the window and swept aside the heavy curtains. Floodlights near the barn pierced the dark night with misty white haloes. Pale patches of snow on the ground were evidence that winter was beginning in the San Luis Valley in southern Colorado. The November night was frigid, which was not unexpected in the largest alpine valley in the world. Cold air from the window swirled around her bare feet. In the distance a coyote hurled his voice skyward in a nocturnal lullaby. The animal yipped dissonantly and then his cry ascended again. Calling his mate or singing for the pure joy of hearing his own voice, he didn't care who heard about his dreams and triumphs. Unlike Stacy Hamelton, who'd locked her childish dreams away in the dark recesses of her mind.

She spread her fingers against the freezing glass. Cold flowed through her hands and up into her arms. A numbing cold. If only it were as easy to numb one's mind. She never should have gone to Mary Beth's wedding. Masochism had never been her favorite indoor sport. So why had she chosen this particular weekend to come home and confront Greg? Her mother would probably insist that it was a subconscious desire to check out the competition, but her mother would be wrong. Those gray eyes of Greg's could smile on any female he wanted.

Mary Beth had glowed beautifully in her bridal white. And the groom...so in love that he could scarcely tear his eyes from his bride. The photographer had ordered everyone hither and yon as if he were stage-managing a play. To get perfect pictures of a perfect day. A tear burned a trail down Stacy's cold cheek. One didn't need photographs. Wedding memories burned themselves into the brain.

Shivering, she dropped the heavy curtain back into place and hastened across the room to her bed. The sheets were icy but eventually her body warmed them and she fell asleep.

An earthquake shattered her dreamworld and dragged her unwillingly from a sound sleep. Stacy forced up reluctant eyelids, blinking to adjust her vision.

"Good morning." Greg's voice came out of the pitch darkness which surrounded her. "Mrs. Ferris."

"What are you doing here?" The room was freezing and she burrowed deeper into the covers.

The mattress abruptly dipped with Greg's weight. "Where should I be, Mrs. Ferris?"

"What time is it?"

"Time for us to talk, Mrs. Ferris."

Yawning, Stacy leaned over and switched on the bedside lamp. Greg was sitting on the edge of her bed wearing his sheepskin coat. She squinted sleepily at her alarm clock. "It's not even five in the morning," she complained. "What's going on?"

"That's a damned good question, Mrs. Ferris."

"What's the matter with you?" The way he kept spitting out "Mrs. Ferris" was getting on her nerves.

"The matter with me?" Greg leaned down, his upper body balanced on arms that fenced her beneath him. "Why should you think something is the matter with me? I apologize for not getting here earlier, Mrs. Ferris, but some horses got loose and one tangled with barbed wire. I had to call Doc for help."

"Was it Rio? Is that why you're upset?"

"Upset?" He drawled the one-word question out thoughtfully. "I guess you could say I'm upset, Mrs.

Ferris. A man comes in after some damned hard work, he likes to have his wife there to ask him how it went. He might even like her to fix him a bite to eat. At least, dammit, he'd like to have his bed warmed."

"What on earth are you talking about?"

"I am talking about, Mrs. Ferris, the fact that suddenly it is common knowledge that apparently you have been Mrs. Gregory Ferris for the past three years."

Stacy was instantly wide-awake. "Lucy Fraser."

"At least you aren't denying you told her we were married."

"I was positive she'd keep her mouth shut. I told her C.B. had tied things up in his will so that you'd lose the ranch if anyone found out you got married before you were thirty-two."

"So Doc informed me. We shared a big laugh over the idea that C.B. would will the ranch away from me for marrying you when everyone in the San Luis Valley knew C.B. adored you. For reasons," he snarled, "which totally escape me."

"I didn't think she'd tell anyone," Stacy said defensively, wishing she could disappear into her pillow as she belatedly recognized Greg's state. Greg Ferris lost his temper maybe once a year and she'd seen grown men quail before the cold fury they'd evoked by beating an animal or mistreating a child. Only once before had Stacy seen that temper directed at her. She attempted appeasement. "Maybe Doc is the only one she told."

"And maybe you've been eating locoweed." Greg rose to his feet and threw her covers to the bottom of the bed. "Get dressed."

"No." Stacy snatched back the covers. Clutching them to her chin, she lay down again. "Go away. We can talk tomorrow."

"It is tomorrow and you have five seconds to get dressed."

"I have no intention of getting up at this hour of the——"

"Four seconds."

"—morning, and, even if I did, there is no way I could possibly get dressed in five——"

"Three seconds."

Her hands tightened around the top edge of the covers. "I don't know what you have in mind, but if you think——"

"Two seconds."

Without relinquishing her death grip on the covers, Stacy scooted to the other side of the bed. "If you don't get out of my bedroom, I'll scream. My father is just down the hall and——"

"One second."

Switching tactics, she gave Greg a tremulous smile. "Why don't you sit down and we'll discuss this? I'm sure we can—— Gregory Ferris, you keep your hands off me!" Too late she remembered that Greg never made idle threats. He struck quickly, rolling her in the covers until she was helpless, her arms pinned to her sides. Stacy let out a piercing scream. Glaring triumphantly at Greg, she waited expectantly for her father to come bursting through her bedroom door. Nothing happened.

Greg gave her a mocking look. "It's very gratifying to know you think I'm a fool, Slim. Did you really think I'd break into this house in the dead of night when I'm well aware that your dad keeps a loaded shotgun handy to scare away predators?"

"Do you mean to tell me that my parents know you are in here abusing me?" Stacy asked indignantly.

"Your parents know that I'm in here discussing matters with my wife," he said with faint emphasis on the last word.

"Oh." She shrunk deep into the mattress. "You told them."

"I told them," he said grimly. "Wouldn't your dad have enjoyed hearing the news in town? His only daughter married for three years and he didn't know a thing about it."

"What did they say?"

"They agreed to let me deal with it. Let's go."

"Go? Just because you have me roped tighter than a maverick calf, you needn't think I'm going anywhere with you." Stacy tried to roll away from him.

Greg gave a harsh laugh and scooped her effortlessly from the bed, one arm behind her back, the other under her knees. "Maybe not willingly, but you're coming."

"I'm not." The tightly wrapped blankets rendered her struggles futile.

Greg wasn't even breathing heavily as he maneuvered her through her bedroom doorway. "Hold still or I'll sling you over my shoulder. Easier for me, but not so comfy for you."

They passed her parents' closed bedroom door. "Help! I'm being kidnapped!" Stacy shrieked.

Her mother stepped into the hall. "Let me open the front door." Ruth Hamelton ran lightly down the staircase. "Be careful you don't fall down the steps, Greg."

"Mother!"

"Yes, dear, I know," her mother said, blinking sleepily. "But you are the one who started this whole mess, aren't you?"

The icy pre-dawn air did nothing to cool Stacy's flaming cheeks. "You told her everything?" she choked out as Greg dropped her on the front seat of his pickup.

He looked up from fastening her seat belt. "I'll be damned if I even know everything. I sure as hell don't know why you told Lucy Fraser we're married."

The pickup door was open and the interior light shone weakly on Greg's face only inches from her own. The flat look in his eyes was a sure sign that he was barely controlling his temper. Greg angry with her was not an experience Stacy relished. In desperation she resorted to tricks she ordinarily despised. Dropping her eyelids, she peered up at him from beneath her lashes. "I did it for you," she said softly. "Don't be mad at me." She should have known better.

"Damn you," Greg said in a tight voice. He clamped her head between his hands, covering her mouth with his in a hard, demanding kiss.

Her head was jammed against the back of the seat, her face tingling beneath the pressure of Greg's cold, work-roughened fingers. His kiss represented something very basic—the age-old conflict between man and woman. Greg wanted her to know his strength and power. She was darned if she would tamely submit. Exerting tremendous effort, she wrenched her face to one side, away from Greg's punishing lips. "Don't," she panted, "you ever kiss me like that." Greg went perfectly still. Swear words rent the cold night air and then he backed out of the truck and slammed the door shut. Stacy shivered with the sudden loss of his body heat. Another blast of cold air assaulted her as Greg opened the other door and slung his long legs under the steering wheel. "I'm cold," she said.

He didn't bother to look at her as he started the engine. "I told you to get dressed." The pickup tore from the driveway with a squeal of tires.

"Well, I didn't and now I'm cold."

"The truck will warm up in a minute." He slammed the gearshift into place.

Stacy clamped her teeth together. She refused to beg or whine. When her chattering teeth were under control, she asked, "Where are we going?"

"Where do you think?" He glanced over at her and frowned. The truck came to a sudden halt on the shoulder of the road. Leaving the engine running, Greg flung off his seat belt and moved toward her. Unsnapping her belt, he pulled her over to the middle of the seat. "You'll get the heat faster here." His voice was curt as if he resented making the concession.

Through the layers of blankets Stacy felt Greg's hands searching for the middle seat belt. Her face was pinned between his head and shoulder as he leaned over her. His jacket collar rubbed against her lips and heat flowed through her body. Greg was right. She was warmer. "Thank you."

Greg tightened the belt across her stomach. "You're welcome." His hard, biting voice clearly conveyed the opposite.

Stacy felt his warm breath on her skin and his face was a pale orb hovering before her eyes. For a long second they seemed frozen in time, two statues staring at each other blindly in the dark. Greg moved closer, touching her mouth with his. His lips were cold and she flinched.

Greg straightened up. Once again the pickup hurtled down the dirt road. Twin headlights pierced the dark pinning a terrified cottontail between their menacing circles. At the last second the rabbit leaped to safety in a white-frosted field. The heavens were cold and sullen-looking with the gray of false dawn. A few tardy stars twinkled brightly. To the east the sky over the Sangre de Cristo Range was rosy with the promise of day. To the west the San Juan Mountains loomed, black and menacing.

As they sped past darkened ranch houses whose occupants still slept, the icy chill that crept up Stacy's spine was caused by more than the November weather. She cleared her throat. "I suppose you think kidnapping me in the middle of the night is going to solve anything?"

"Probably not, but dragging you from your warm bed was damned satisfying."

"Throwing a temper tantrum isn't like you," Stacy said.

"What the hell did you think I'd do when I found out?"

"I didn't think you'd find out."

"That was your first mistake."

Not her first. "All right. Telling Lucy Fraser we're married was a big mistake. My mistake. Are you satisfied?"

"No."

"I admitted I made a mistake," Stacy said. "What do you want from me? Sackcloth and ashes?"

"I want to know why you did it."

"That makes two of us," she said unhappily.

"Drop the pathetic little act, Slim. It won't cut any ice with me. You always know exactly what you're doing."

"All right," Stacy said, driven to tell the truth. "Lucy Fraser is a ninny."

"What's that to you?" The pickup careened around a corner on two wheels.

Stacy took a deep breath. "Lucy Fraser practically admitted she was planning to become Mrs. Gregory Ferris."

"And you object to that?"

"C.B. said if people were as careful picking their partners in life as they were in breeding their cattle, the world would be a better place. He also said ranch women ought to be able to pull their own weight and city women should stick to city men." She slanted a glance at Greg. "He told me your dad might have settled down on the ranch except for your mom."

"C.B.'s opinion of my parents' life-style and divorce was not exactly a highly guarded secret." With a violent yank, Greg shifted into a lower gear as they turned under the high gate that marked the entrance to Greg's ranch.

"Don't you see? Lucy Fraser is all wrong for you."

An endless moment passed before Greg asked, "I'm supposed to believe you were saving me from Lucy for my own good?"

"All she was interested in was your rampant masculinity. She practically slobbered when she talked about your bottom."

"Is that what set you off? The thought that another woman might find me attractive?"

"I told you——"

"You haven't told me anything but a bunch of half-baked garbage. You don't give a damn whom I marry and we both know it." With a spray of gravel the pickup came to a halt. Greg turned to face Stacy, his voice harsh with anger. "You told Lucy we were married for no other reason than sheer malice."

"Malice! I like that! I——"

"No, you don't. No one likes to hear the truth about herself." Greg jumped down from the pickup. Opening the door on her side, he added, "Least of all you."

"Look who's talking. You wouldn't recognize the truth about you if it bit you on the—— Gregory Ferris, what are you doing? Put me down this instant." Stacy heaved her body but her efforts were restricted by the blankets. An owl hooted derisively from the old cottonwood tree near the corner of the house.

Greg slammed the truck door and carried her up the few steps to his front door. "Quit wiggling. If I drop you or bang your head on the doorframe, it will be your own damned fault."

"I want you to take me home right this instant."

Greg kicked the door shut behind him. "I hope this doesn't come as a big shock, but I don't give a damn what you want."

"Gregory Ferris, don't you dare take me up to your bedroom!"

He mounted the wide staircase. "You're the one who announced we're married."

"That doesn't give you the right to——"

"Bed my wife?"

One bulb was burning in the upstairs hallway and its feeble glow cast strange shadows on Greg's face. Twin obelisks of reflected light glowed demonically in dark eyes. Stacy was icy cold inside the tunnel of blanket. "I don't want you to."

Greg shouldered open a door. "I know that." He dumped her on a bed. "We'll talk later."

The room was dark. Stacy struggled to loosen the blankets. "What do you mean, we'll talk later?"

"I mean, we'll talk later," he said evenly. "I'm too tired and too angry to deal with this mess now."

She momentarily abandoned her struggles. "What am I supposed to do? Hang around until it's convenient for you?"

"That will do for a start."

"I have no intention of hanging around. I want to go home."

"You made your bed, Mrs. Ferris. Now you can damned well sleep in it."

The blankets were suffocating her. "You take me home right this instant, Gregory Ferris, or I'm going to take your pickup and drive myself home."

"I wouldn't if I were you." He stood beside the bed, silhouetted by the hall light.

"Well, you're not me, are you?"

"No, I'm seven inches taller, outweigh you by a considerable amount and I'm a whole lot tougher than you'll ever be."

There wasn't a hint of threat or boastfulness in Greg's voice, which didn't mean he wasn't serious. Freeing one arm, Stacy propped herself up on her elbow. Her low vantage point created the illusion that Greg was ten feet tall. For the first time, she felt a tiny stab of fear. "You can't make me stay."

"You know better than that." The low, drawled words were wrapped around a core of steel.

Stacy weighed her chances of escape. Enshrouded in the blankets, she was as securely caught as a trout on a hook. Even if she could wriggle free, Greg would be on her in a minute. And there was no denying that Greg could overpower her in a fair fight. Which was why she had no intention of fighting fair. She'd leave as soon as Greg went to sleep. He always left his keys in his pickup. By the time he discovered her absence, she'd be on her way back to Colorado Springs. Once Greg had cooled off they could discuss the situation on her terms. In her territory.

"Well?" Greg asked impatiently. "Are you ready to stay or do you need a little more convincing?"

"You'd like an excuse to play caveman, wouldn't you?"

"Actually, I believe I would." He stepped toward the bed.

"Forget it," Stacy snapped, detecting a hint of amusement in Greg's voice. Kidnapping her was bad enough, but laughing at her inability to strike back was infuriating. She glared up at him. "You win." For now, she added silently.

"Giving up? I never thought I'd hear that from you, Slim."

"I am not giving up. There's no point in wasting my breath discussing anything with someone who's childishly and stubbornly refusing to listen to reason. Maybe a few hours' sleep will put you in a more rational frame of mind."

"How very sensible of you, Mrs. Ferris." His voice mocked her haughty tones. "A good night's sleep will do us both good."

"You can't sleep with me." She was determined to have the last word.

"I have no intention of sleeping with you. That's why you're in the spare bedroom. Pleasant dreams, Mrs. Ferris." The bedroom door closed firmly behind him.

"Bully!" she hollered. A smothered laugh was her only answer. Furiously Stacy fought free of the imprisoning blankets and crawled beneath the bed sheets. She'd give Greg time to fall asleep and then she'd leave. Slowly the bed lost its icy chill and her eyelids dropped shut. Gregory Ferris was going to be sorry he started this.

She'd been prepared to be reasonable, but if it was war he wanted . . .

Morning sun flooded the room as Stacy slowly awakened. Bright pink walls assaulted her and she quickly closed her eyes. Barely reopening them, she took a second look. No modernistic nightmare surrounded her but the spare bedroom that she and C.B. had decorated over a dozen years ago for Greg's mother when Julia Ferris visited the ranch. Stacy's gaze traveled over garish walls and huge fuchsia tulips on the chartreuse curtains and overstuffed chair. She'd been so proud of that fabric when she'd helped C.B. select it. Now she winced, her gaze moving on. Lace covered every flat surface in the room, Stacy having been convinced at the time that city women couldn't live without lace. Saccharine pictures punctuated the walls. Young blue-eyed girls with improbable blond curls. Enough puppies and kittens to supply every child in the San Luis Valley with a pet. A pint-size shepherdess dressed impeccably in white smiled on her flock of equally impeccably white lambs. Greg had heaped bushels of scorn on that picture, but she and C.B. had been decorating this room and Greg's opinion . . .

Greg. The events of the past evening flooded back with total recall. How could she have fallen asleep? And she called Lucy Fraser a ninny. At least Lucy Fraser hadn't got herself into a situation where a raging maniac hauled her out of bed and dumped her in his. Well, his spare bed. Stacy didn't even have anything to wear besides her pajamas. Breathing fire like an avenging angel rather lost its effect when one was wearing pajamas. It was a wonder Greg hadn't hauled her out of bed to fix his breakfast. That was the brutish kind of activity he seemed currently to be indulging in. Maybe he was still in bed.

Searching for a clock, Stacy rolled over. And forgot to breathe. Stacked neatly against the opposite wall were her suitcase and bag. The open wardrobe door revealed her clothing. She bolted from the bed. In the bathroom that connected the room she was in with Greg's old bedroom were her cosmetics and beauty aids lined up with military precision. Her red toothbrush hung over the sink. A green toothbrush hung companionably beside it.

Even as she jerked open the door in the opposite wall, Stacy knew what she was going to see. Greg hadn't moved into his uncle's vacant bedroom. She was unprepared for the painful rush of nostalgia at the sight of a room she hadn't stepped foot in for three years. Nothing had changed. Stacy's mother had made the blue denim curtains while the old Pendleton blankets had come from a long-forgotten ancestor of C.B.'s. Stacy knew if she looked in the bookshelves lining the far wall she'd find many old friends. Thumb-tacked over the other three walls were hundreds of photographs taken by Greg over the years. Surprise jolted through her body as she looked at the nearest wall and her own face, albeit younger, stared back at her. Without stopping for slippers or robe, she headed downstairs.

She found him in C.B.'s old office. His dusty boots on C.B.'s scarred old desk, leaning back in C.B.'s worn leather chair, Greg held a stack of papers in one hand and a pencil in the other. He was sound asleep. Stacy tiptoed backward from the room and quietly closed the door. Greg must have fetched her things after she'd gone to sleep. Unless her mother had brought them. What must her parents think? She ought to call them. No. Her parents' behavior last night made it very clear this was between Greg and Stacy.

And Stacy intended to settle it her way. Catching Greg asleep was an unforeseen bit of luck. She climbed two stairs before an ill-timed sense of fair play made her reluctantly turn and head back down the staircase. Sneaking out earlier in the heat of battle was one thing, but it didn't seem quite fair to take advantage of Greg now. There were new lines in his forehead, the creases beside his mouth were deeper, the lines around his eyes more pronounced. His cheeks were windburned. He looked exhausted and unexpectedly vulnerable.

The dining room was another page from the past. Only in the kitchen had any changes been made. The Ferris men were hard on coffeepots and an unfamiliar one was no surprise. The microwave was. C.B. had grumbled that at his age he didn't need any newfangled gadgets shooting him with X rays. A note on the coffee maker said "Juice in frig. Eggs in micro. Hit start." Stacy hit the start button. A ping later, sipping orange juice, she pulled steaming hot scrambled eggs from the microwave, a cheesy smell permeating the kitchen. Suddenly ravenous, she grabbed a plate and eating utensils from the cupboard. They were exactly where they'd always been.

"Still here, I see."

Her mouth filled with eggs, Stacy looked up to see Greg standing in the doorway. "After the way you treated me last night, I figured you owed me breakfast before I left."

Greg poured himself a mug of coffee and leaned against the counter. Tilting his head back, he drank deeply. "I needed that." He rubbed his face as if he were still waking up.

A guilty qualm struck Stacy but she ruthlessly shoved it aside. "You wouldn't look like death warmed over if you'd spend the night in your bed instead of tearing around the countryside kidnapping innocent maidens." Maybe not totally innocent, but certainly innocent of the kind of ridiculous charges Greg had flung around.

"Some things are more important than sleep." He drained his mug and refilled it.

"Afraid I'd run out on you if you shut your eyes?"

"Nope." He pulled a chair out from the table and turned it around, straddling it with his arms across the back.

"I suppose you thought your stupid threats would keep me in line." She pulled toast from the toaster.

Greg sipped his coffee, studying her over the top of his mug. "I don't remember making any threats."

"You were too clever to put anything into words. You just relied on your usual ugly, menacing air."

"I remember you shaking in your boots." He dipped his head and looked under the table.

Stacy tucked her bare feet behind the legs of her chair. "I wasn't shaking with fear. Any shaking was because you dragged me out into the dead of winter. I'll be lucky if I don't die of pneumonia. And fear has nothing to do with me still being here."

"I know that. Sneaking out while I slept would be taking unfair advantage. You want to best me, but you'd never cheat."

She scowled across the table. "It's not cheating when you're a sidewinding skunk who's lower than a snake's belly."

"Then why are you still here?"

"I was hungry, so I'm eating breakfast." She chewed a forkful of eggs. "I'll leave when I'm good and ready."

"Quite a change in attitude from last night when you begged to go home."

"I did not beg. I merely stated my wishes. Once I was settled here in bed, I saw no reason to let the fact that you are a Neanderthal cretin force me out into the cold night again."

"My, what big words," Greg mocked. "You city girls can shur talk purdy."

"And you country boys can act like the hind ends of mules."

"Never at a loss for words." Greg saluted her with his mug. "Which is, I believe, exactly what got you into this mess."

"I wasn't aware that I am in a mess."

"No?" Greg arched an eyebrow. "I've had six phone calls this morning offering congratulation and two wondering if I think a bridal shower three years after the fact is too late."

Stacy wrinkled her nose in disgust. "What did Lucy Fraser do? Put it on the radio? You must have given that schoolteacher plenty of reason to believe becoming Mrs. Gregory Ferris was hers for the asking. She's certainly behaving like a woman scorned. I can't see any other reason for her blabbing news that I made very clear was ruinous to you if it got out."

"She asked Darrel Epson if it was true that C.B.'s will prohibited me from marrying before I was thirty-two."

"Of all the nerve." Stacy slapped her spoon on the table. "Can you believe the gall of that woman, thinking I'm a liar?"

"Imagine that."

"I admit I bent the truth a little, but little white lies are perfectly permissible if they're for a good cause."

"Don't try and pass that cockeyed notion off as something you learned from C.B." Greg looked her squarely in the face. "And I don't want to hear any more lies or feeble explanations. I want the truth and I want it now."

Greg's earlier grand temper might have been brought under control but his anger still lay too near the surface for Stacy's peace of mind. "What do you want to know?" she asked.

They were both fully aware she knew perfectly well the answer to that, but Greg answered her anyway. "I want to know why, after we've kept our marriage secret for three years, you suddenly felt compelled to announce to the whole world that you're my wife."

CHAPTER THREE

"MAYBE I was tired of living a lie."

"Maybe."

"Don't give me that arrogant, skeptical look, Gregory Ferris. I know what you're thinking and I did not blurt out about our marriage because of jealousy. I told you last——"

"And I told you," Greg said evenly. "I don't want any more bedtime stories. I want the truth."

"The truth is..." Stacy poked at her eggs with her fork.

"The truth is, Mrs. Ferris?"

"Quit sounding like an old-fashioned schoolmarm. And quit calling me Mrs. Ferris in that odious tone of voice." Mrs. Gregory Ferris. The name had been a reverse talisman over the past three years. When life was tough, reciting the name unleashed an angry strength that served Stacy well. "Mrs. Gregory Ferris."

"Nice name."

She hadn't meant to say the words out loud. "My own private swear words."

"Lucky you." His faint smile was more grimace. "At least you had an outlet for your frustration."

She felt the heat redden her face as his meaning sunk in. "I suppose I never considered that. I never expected that you wouldn't... I mean... It must have been difficult for you."

"Difficult?" Greg took a long swallow of coffee. "Married, but not married. Forced to keep the situation

44

a secret. Unable to do anything about it. At least you escaped.''

"Escaped?" Stacy tore her toast into little pieces. "I'd hardly call it escaping when every letter from my mother was filled with 'Greg this' and 'Greg that.'"

"All you had to do was throw out the letters. Your folks, C.B.—I saw them almost every day." He stood up and walked over to the coffeepot and refilled his mug. "You heard your dad last night. That was mild. Lately he's been pushing hard."

"I've tried to tell them that you and I aren't interested, but they just don't listen." She pushed the litter of crumbs into a pile. "It's as if they've made up their minds that I'm going to marry you and my feelings don't matter."

"And you thought announcing to the world that we're already married would shut them up."

Irritation flared at his sarcastic drawl. "I didn't announce anything. I merely made one small comment to your precious Lucy Fraser. She's the one who blabbed."

"Lucy only repeated what you told her."

"Oh, sure. Exonerate your precious Lucy Fraser."

"Quit calling her my precious Lucy Fraser."

"Well, she's certainly not *my* precious Lucy Fraser," Stacy retorted. "If you want to know what I think——"

"I don't."

"—she's a real pain in the neck."

"I might have known," Greg said censoriously. "Lucy made a few innocent remarks and you leaped in feet— or should I say, mouth?—first."

"I don't know why you always blame everything on me." Stacy stood up and took her dirty dishes to the sink.

"I don't blame everything on you. I was old enough to know better than to take an inexperienced baby like you to bed."

His calling her a baby stung. "Yes, you were." She swung angrily around. "Instead of acting like an over-sexed Sir Galahad, you should have taken me straight home to my parents."

Greg's eyes narrowed. "You might remember that the reason we're in this ridiculous situation is because you flagged me down on the road to C.B.'s."

She thrust her plate into the dishwasher. "You didn't have to stop."

"I thought your damned car had broken down. Was I supposed to drive right on by?"

"Yes." Gregory Ferris could no more drive by a person or animal in trouble than a river could climb mountains.

"You were crying."

"You forgot my twenty-first birthday." She'd looked forward to the day for weeks. It was intended to be a celebration of the fact that she'd grown up.

"I had plans that night. I intended to give you your present the next day. We've been over this before and it changes nothing." After a moment, he added, "You don't know how often I've cursed the fates for that night."

"The fates or me?" She scrubbed a spot on the countertop.

"Both," he said harshly. "You were such a baby. Insisting I make a woman of you."

"If I was such a baby, you should have turned me down." She viciously squeezed the dish sponge.

"Along with all your other faults, you seem to have a convenient memory. You know damned good and well the only reason I made love to you was because you swore if I didn't you'd find someone who would.''

His words were no less infuriating for being the truth. The truth as Greg knew it. ''The only reason you made love to me is because you'd been partying and you were liquored up enough that you'd have made love to a fence post and you know it.''

''I probably would have enjoyed it more. At least a fence post wouldn't have cried the entire time.''

''It wasn't exactly heaven on earth for me either.'' Stacy's shrill words reverberated through the kitchen. The loud ticking of the clock on the stove beat against her skull. A stray sunbeam produced a rainbow of colors on the greasy water in the sink. The same colors that haunted her dreams. Garish colors flashing on a dirty motel wall from the neon sign across the street that had blinked relentlessly on and off. Her breakfast threatened to come up. She swallowed hard. ''On Monday I'll see a lawyer about a divorce.''

''Don't you think it might be a bit awkward to explain why you're getting a divorce so soon after spilling the news that we're married and have been for three years?''

''I'll think of something.''

''I can hardly wait to hear what.''

Stacy bit her lower lip. Greg was as deep in this muddle as she was, a fact that didn't seem to occur to him any more than helping her out did. Taking a deep breath, she faced him. ''We can tell everyone we didn't want to hurt C.B. by getting a divorce but now...'' Pain had to be conquered before she could continue. ''Now he's dead, we don't have to worry about that.''

''How does it happen we were married in the first place?''

Stacy forced herself not to crumble before Greg's cool gaze. "Youthful spirits." She shrugged. "It was never any secret that I was crazy about you when I was younger."

"I suppose I took advantage of that to haul you to a justice of the peace. Why did we keep it a secret and live apart?"

"I don't know. I was in college and you wanted me to quit and we fought..." A flash of anger in Greg's eyes silenced her.

"Let me get this straight. I took advantage of your youthful crush and then tried to stand in the way of your girlish ambitions. Did I leave anything out? Perhaps rape on our wedding night which sent you screaming into the night and fleeing from the Valley to hide in the big city? Maybe we can tell everyone that I've been sitting around gloating over my land and cows while my wife was living in city slums working her fingers to the bone and barely keeping her head above the poverty level. What the hell," he added in a weary voice, "throw in a few broken bones and bruises. Make me a wife beater."

"All right, you don't have to be so darned sarcastic." She eyed him cautiously. Greg Ferris losing his temper twice in two days would be some kind of record. "Even if I did say that, not one person in the San Luis Valley would believe me. Beating me would take more energy and emotion than you're capable of."

"I don't know. I imagine I could work up a little sweat if you annoyed me enough."

"Ha. You hardly batted an eye when I hysterically insisted you had to marry me. When I told you I was going back to college and never wanted to see you again, you didn't even bother to look up from the fence wire you were stringing."

"Did you want me to stop you?" His eyes bored into her.

"Of course not. You couldn't have."

There was a short pause. "I thought you knew me better than that," Greg said finally.

Meaning he could have stopped her if he'd wanted to. Which he definitely had not. The knowledge shouldn't hurt, but it did. "I'll take care of getting our divorce."

"No, you won't."

"This stupid marriage was all my fault. I admit it, and I intend to pay for the divorce." His earlier accusation that she'd behaved childishly still rankled and she rushed to add, "I haven't accepted one dime from you since we got married and I don't intend to start now. I have no intention of being any further in your debt or listening to you go on and on about how the marriage was my fault but you got stuck paying for the divorce. You can just——"

"There isn't going to be a divorce."

Greg's flat statement flabbergasted Stacy and she stared at him in stunned disbelief, her mouth agape. "Of course there is," she finally managed. Leaning back against the cabinets, she caught at the countertop edge behind her. "You said last night..." Comprehension flashed into her head. "I get it. Just because I let you kiss me last night and then said one silly, stupid thing to a ditsy female who no more belongs on a ranch than knapweed, you've taken some idiotic notion into that thick head of yours that I want to stay married to you. Well, you can just forget that right now. There is no one on this entire earth who will be more thrilled than me when we get a divorce."

"A thrill that will be somewhat postponed, I'm afraid."

"You needn't be afraid of anything, because it's not going to be postponed," Stacy said doggedly. "I'm going straight back to Colorado Springs and the first thing tomorrow morning I'm going to phone a lawyer and there's nothing you can do about it."

"I wouldn't count on that, Mrs. Ferris."

"Quit calling me Mrs. Ferris and quit uttering empty threats in that toneless voice that's supposed to scare the pants off me. It might have worked when I was eight or ten, but I'm twenty-four now and I won't be threatened."

"A divorce doesn't happen to be in the books at the moment," Greg said evenly. "You're Mrs. Gregory Ferris and you're going to stay that way until I decide otherwise."

"I have news for you, Gregory Ferris. This is the twentieth century and I don't need your permission to get a divorce. You can't keep me a prisoner here on your ranch. Go ahead and contest the divorce. It's your money. You'll be making a fool of yourself and it won't do you any good."

"I'll contest the divorce. In court and out. I can see the headlines now. About how you begged me to make love to you. How I, the all-American boy, held out until you threatened me with falling into bed with the first male that came along."

"You wouldn't." She gripped the edge of the counter top so fiercely that her fingers hurt.

He went on as if she hadn't spoken. "How you came crying to me that you were pregnant and I gallantly married you. How I wanted to go to your parents but you..." He gave her a mocking look. "Your mother would love to read that you were afraid to tell them. People will wonder why you were afraid of them."

"I wasn't afraid of them and you know it. I thought if we told them we were married before I told them I was pregnant they wouldn't be so disappointed. Okay, so I wasn't thinking straight. I was a little upset, if you'll remember," she added angrily.

"We're not talking about what I remember. We're talking about the kind of innuendo I can smear all over the newspapers."

"Why are you against the divorce?" This cold, hurtful stranger wasn't the Gregory Ferris she'd grown up around. "Why do you want to be tied to a woman who——"

"Hates me?"

His dispassionate voice demonstrated a complete lack of interest in her answer, but she considered the question all the same. For sixteen years she'd loved Greg. A silly, childish infatuation that would have withered away with the passage of time. Only it hadn't been allowed to wither; it was cruelly yanked from her heart the day she'd married Greg. He had taken her innocence and her love, leaving in return a cold anger that had sustained her for the past three years. Last night she'd determined to rid herself of that anger. Now was a good time to start.

"No," she said slowly. "That is, at times I have, but it doesn't matter any more. We have to think of the future. You've got Lucy Fraser waiting in the wings and I——"

"Yes, I'm curious, Slim. Who's the Prince Charming who sent you back to the Valley begging for freedom?"

"I'm not begging. I'm telling you. I'm getting a divorce."

"Go ahead."

"You won't stop me," she said with relief. Greg had only been exacting petty revenge.

"I told you what I'll do." The words were drawled in a softly spoken, utterly inflexible voice.

Dismay, fury and frustration clashed within Stacy. "Damn you, Gregory Ferris. What do you want from me?"

Greg rose to his full height and looked across the room at her. A long moment passed before he spoke. "I want this marriage business between us finished."

Stacy was confused. "I told you I'd get a divorce."

Shaking his head, Greg started from the kitchen. "Not that way. I want it to end the way it began. I won't contest the divorce . . ." He turned in the doorway to look at her, a considering look upon his face.

An ominous foreboding invaded her spine. "If?"

"Not if. When. When you sleep with me again."

Stunned, Stacy stared blankly at the empty doorway. Either Greg had gone completely, utterly insane or her ears had deceived her. She rushed after him. He was in the front hall. "Greg, wait. What did you just say?"

"You heard me." He shrugged into his jacket and reached for his hat. "You want a divorce, you can get it, Mrs. Ferris—the hard way or the easy way. The hard way, I'll contest it. I'll fight you every step of the way. I'll make sure that every titillating detail is splashed all over the newspapers."

"And the easy way?" she breathed.

Greg set his hat on his head. "Sleep with me. Once. Then you can get your divorce and I won't contest it."

"Easy? That's your idea of easy?" Her voice rose in horror. "You're crazy if you think I'd consider sleeping with you." Greg stood patiently at the front door, his hand on the handle. "This is your idea of revenge, isn't it? I not only screwed up your life by forcing you to marry me, I attacked your manhood when I said making love with you wasn't wonderful. Making love!'' she choked, clenching her fists at her sides. "What a laugh. As if love had anything to do with it. I know why you're doing this. You think you can prove what a great lover you are. You're wrong. I'll find the experience every bit as unsatisfactory as I did the last time I went to bed with you.''

"You won't, but that's beside the point. Sleep with me once and the divorce is yours. You have my word on it.''

"No.'' She looked with outrage at his outstretched hand. "I don't make deals with the devil. As soon as I get back to Colorado Springs I'm going to a lawyer and there's nothing you can do about it.''

"You'd be surprised what I can do.''

"Nothing about you would surprise me. Go ahead. Do your worst. Publish and be damned. Spread every last sordid detail of our silly little tryst in the papers. I couldn't care less.''

"An opinion your parents will share, I'm sure.''

Her stomach clenched as if he'd punched her. "You'd do that to them?''

"The choice is up to you, a city gal with big city values. You've probably forgotten how it is in a small town. Maybe you don't care if your folks would be so shamed they'd sell out and leave the Valley and go off to Arizona or somewhere. They'd probably die away from the ranch. Leaving you their money. A damned good plan. One almost admires you for it.''

"You monster,'' she whispered. "To think I worshiped you.'' Tears stung her eyes. "I looked up to you. I should have looked down, and seen your feet of clay.'' Rising hysteria clawed at her throat. "I won't do it, do you hear me? I won't!''

"You don't need to decide this minute. Think about it."

"I don't need to think about it. After all you've said, even you can't expect me to tamely march upstairs and fall into your bed and welcome you with open arms. I'd throw up."

Greg laughed. "Knowing you, you would if you had to stick your finger down your throat to do it. I'm not unreasonable. I won't even insist on an answer this weekend. I've waited three years—I can wait until you're ready to come to my bed."

"I'll never be ready for that."

He shrugged. "It all depends on how badly you want to be free, doesn't it?"

"That's a stiff price to pay for freedom."

Greg pulled his hat low over his forehead. "Our marriage cost me dearly. Why should the divorce come any cheaper?" The door closed firmly behind him.

Stacy crossed the floor on shaking legs and dropped down on the wooden staircase. The cold draught that had entered with Greg's departure clutched at her ankles. Even after three years of estrangement it was impossible to believe that their friendship had degenerated into this hateful need for revenge.

She cast her mind back to the past. Greg had moved to the upper San Luis Valley when he was fourteen and she was eight. His parents were undergoing a messy divorce and they'd removed Greg from the shrieking headlines, sending him to live with C.B. Ferris, his father's uncle. Greg's mother was a leading actress on the New York stage and his father a roving newspaperman. When the dust of their divorce settled, the only two things they had agreed on were that they couldn't live with each other and Greg was better off on the ranch than with either of them. A decision that had suited C.B. and Greg just fine, because by then each had taken the other's measure and a deep love and respect between the two had begun to grow and flourish.

A city boy, Greg had been the rawest tenderfoot. His clothes were wrong, his speech was funny, he'd never ridden a horse and he thought every animal with horns and four hoofs was a bull. But Greg had watched and worked hard and learned. By the time he was eighteen he had been a top cowhand. Four years of college had added bulk to his lean body and the business knowledge necessary for successfully managing a large ranch. It was no secret that C.B., a bachelor, considered Greg his surrogate son. By the time Greg was twenty-four there wasn't a man in the Valley who didn't respect Greg's knowledge, judgment and ability. And not a woman who didn't appreciate his slow smiles and wide shoulders.

Stacy was no exception. She'd handed Greg her heart on a silver platter. Curling her fingers around a banister pillar, Stacy pressed her forehead against the chilly wood. What an innocent she'd been. When she was ten and Greg sixteen, she'd asked him to marry her. Any other teenage boy would have laughed at the childish question, but Greg had seriously turned the matter over in his mind before saying it was fine with him but he thought they ought to wait until Stacy grew up. Stacy had made him promise and then she'd considered the matter settled.

In high school she had clung to her dream. Hidden away in her bureau were pictures of bridal gowns, hints on planning the perfect wedding and descriptions of honeymoon locations. Greg had gone off to college and each time he returned to the Valley, she'd reminded him of his promise and each time he'd said he was waiting for her to grow up. When she'd finished high school,

he'd encouraged her to attend the university. Her room-
mates had laughingly called her the oldest virgin in
Colorado but she hadn't cared. She was saving herself
for marriage and Greg.

Then had come her fateful twenty-first birthday. Half
expecting an engagement ring from Greg, she'd been
devastated when he hadn't even made an appearance.
For the first time she'd realized that her dream wasn't
Greg's. That all those years he'd been humoring her, as
one humored a child. The painful knowledge had sent
her in search of Greg the minute her parents had gone
to bed. Fueled as much by anger as self-pity, she'd determined to force him into acknowledging that she'd
grown up at last.

Stacy clamped her eyelids tightly shut. Tears were as
useless as wishing she'd never been so rash and stupid.
Wishing couldn't change the past. She'd forced Greg to
sleep with her, she'd thought she was pregnant and he'd
married her.

Stacy had insisted they be married secretly away from
the Valley. Greg had driven blindly over Wolf Creek Pass
in a torrential downpour. She'd cried, half scared they
were going to die and half wishing she would. Greg
hadn't spoken to her all the way to Durango where they'd
mumbled hasty words before a judge.

When she'd thought it could get no worse... Stacy
clutched at the banister with deadened fingers. If she
lived to be a hundred she'd never forget the look of disbelief on Greg's face when she had come out of the
ladies' room at the gas station in Pagosa Springs two
hours after the wedding and told him she wasn't pregnant
after all. In her fear and inexperience she'd simply mis-
calculated. Greg's disbelief had quickly turned to accusation and then to rage such as she'd never seen him

exhibit before. His horrid, slashing words had carved themselves on her heart. For the first time in her life she'd feared Greg and he'd seen that fear on her face and, seeing it, his rage had turned cold. Bitter cold, like dry ice, so cold she'd turned into a frozen lump with singed edges. At that moment Stacy had entered adulthood. Gone forever were the dreams and hopes of childhood, to be replaced by the terrible knowledge that Greg not only didn't return her love, but despised her for the predicament into which she'd pitchforked him.

Trembling from the aftershocks of spent emotion, Stacy felt ill. Greg hadn't forgiven her. He never threatened with meaningless words. He'd do what he promised. To ruthlessly sacrifice her parents, his good friends, on the altar of his revenge he must hate her enormously. If only he'd raged at her. Anything was better than him standing there stating his condition as calmly as if he were reciting the weather report. She shivered; her skin felt cold and clammy. Opening her eyes, she realized with some surprise that she was still wearing her pajamas. No wonder she was cold.

Upstairs in the spare bedroom Stacy unfolded a pair of worn jeans from her suitcase. She'd find Greg and attempt to reason with him. The buttons on her pajama top defied fumbling fingers. Last night she'd accused him of being a granite rock. Granite was soft compared to Greg. Pleading, tears, bargaining, reasoning... Reasoning. Who was she trying to fool? One could more easily reason with the Rio Grande during the spring floods than change Greg's mind when he'd determined a path of action. Except that normally Greg didn't deliberately set out to hurt. Once again he was making an exception in her case. It wasn't enough that three years ago he'd rejected her as ruthlessly as he'd toss aside a noxious weed. It wasn't enough that he'd broken her heart and crushed her self-esteem. That she had loved him had never exonerated her in his eyes. She no longer loved him, but he still blamed her for the mess she'd embroiled him in. Blamed her, hated her and wanted his revenge.

She crossed the icy wooden floor and pushed aside the curtains at the window. Greg walked out of a small shed and looked up. Their eyes locked across the ranch yard and a cold dread clutched at Stacy's stomach. Greg's gaze was steady and uncompromising. As clearly as if he'd shouted the words Stacy knew that Greg was reminding her of his ultimatum. The next move was hers. The curtains fell, severing the hold his gaze had on her. If only it were as easy to sever their marriage. Stacy crushed the curtain fabric in her hand. She had to try.

Jeans were a mistake and she ripped them from her body. Starry-eyed country girls wore jeans and were easily intimidated by tall, lanky men who oozed masculinity. City women girded themselves in silks and woolens and eyed macho cowboys with just the right amount of amused tolerance.

Greg had disappeared by the time Stacy walked out the back door, dropping her luggage on the porch. Dan Goodwinn hailed her as she crossed the yard. "I should have known you were around, the way this fellow was acting." Greg's foreman nodded in the direction of the corral.

"How are you, Dan?" Switching directions, she headed toward the corral where the stocky man was closing the gate and a magnificent sorrel stallion stood, his head erect, his ears pricked in her direction. "What's Rio doing up at the house?"

"He's getting new shoes in the morning."

The large red horse nickered a soft greeting as Stacy stepped up on the bottom rail of the corral. "Yes, I love you, too," she crooned. Grasping the stallion's halter, she held his head still and blew into his nostrils, laughing when he snorted in her face. Rio turned his head slightly to study her with one large hazel eye. Stacy climbed up another rail and leaned over to work her fingers through Rio's mane. "Who would guess you're eighteen years old?"

"He's getting a few gray hairs around his muzzle," Dan said, "but his memory is holding good. He sure knew you right off."

Stacy laughed as the horse nibbled her shoulder. "This jacket cost me a small fortune, you pop-eyed, sway-backed, knock-kneed excuse for a horse." Since the remark was uttered in a caressing voice, the horse ignored the unwarranted slurs on his appearance.

"Hard to believe he's the same horse Greg trucked home to C.B. fourteen years ago," the foreman said. "That was the first time I ever saw Greg in a temper. Not that I blamed him. Rio was nothing but bone and skin and whip marks."

"I remember. Who would have thought starving to death was your bit of luck, fellow?" Stacy worked her way up and down the crest of Rio's neck. "If you hadn't broken down your fence to get to some grass, you wouldn't have been stumbling along the highway where Greg found you."

"And lucky that Greg was hauling an empty horse trailer."

"I still think C.B. should have shot Rio's owner instead of paying him for Rio," Stacy said.

"C.B. could have taken it to the authorities, but he figured buying the horse was the quickest way to get Rio help," Dan said. "You can bet C.B. put the fear of God in the fellow. He made him sign a statement saying he'd never own another animal, and don't think C.B. didn't keep an eye on him."

Stacy blinked back tears at the memory. "I was here when Greg drove up. When he led Rio down the trailer ramp..."

"Yeah, I remember you sobbing while the horse stood there with his eyes shut and every part of his body drooping."

C.B. had wanted to call the vet to put the animal down, but Greg had fought to save the horse and C.B. had reluctantly given in, cautioning Greg that all the best intentions couldn't work miracles. Secretly, Stacy had agreed with C.B. that the horse wouldn't live the night, but because by then she was ten years old and considered herself in love with Greg she'd stoutly upheld Greg's argument. The two of them had spent the night in the barn with Rio, Greg alternately raging at the horse's former owner and gently treating the horse's wounds. Ill to the point of apathy, Rio had made no objection to the two of them touching him.

It wasn't until the horse had healed that everyone realized the true extent of the damage. Rio hated humans with every inch of his filling-out body. When his more experienced uncle shook his head and said the horse would never be anything but a crazed killer, Greg, who'd only lived on the ranch two years, dug in his heels and insisted he could tame the beast within Rio. Against his better judgment, C.B. had given in to his nephew's entreaty.

It had taken two years but at the end of that time Rio had gone from an enraged beast to barnyard pet, following Greg around like an oversize puppy dog, responsive to Greg's quiet commands and light touch, all this accomplished without Greg ever raising his voice or punishing Rio in any way. In the battle waged between man and horse, patience and determination were Greg's weapons and he'd used them with great skill. Stacy remembered her mother once saying that Greg had more patience than any ten other men combined. She would do well to remember that.

Rio stuck his head in her chest and pushed against her. "What do you want, you greedy creature? Aren't I paying enough attention to you?" Rio brought up his head, and stared over her shoulder, his head and ears alert, his tail held high. Stacy didn't need to turn to know that Greg had walked up behind her.

"He probably wants an apple," Greg said.

Stacy concentrated on combing her fingers through Rio's mane. "Don't tell me you've taught him to pan-handle apples."

"Not me." Greg held out an apple. "Here."

Stacy accepted the apple without looking at Greg. Rio took it delicately from her open hand, his lips brushing her palm.

"I suppose now that you two are admitting you're married, you won't have to sneak Rio his apples, Stacy."

Ignoring her flaming cheeks at Dan's mention of their marriage, Stacy said, "I don't know what you mean."

"It got to be a game with the hands," Dan explained. "First one to see you give ol' Rio here an apple won a beer. If we heard you was back, we'd watch the near pasture for your car."

Stacy turned indignantly to Greg. "You had them spy on me?"

"A temporary hand, not from around here, saw you with Rio and reported it. He didn't know who you were.

Naturally I checked on what strange woman was giving apples to my horse.''

"Don't know why you had to check," Dan chuckled. "This old fleabag wouldn't give the time of day to any other woman. He'll be happy she's finally coming back here where she belongs."

Stacy stepped down from the corral bars. "Cupboard love. Rio's a sucker for anyone with an apple."

"You know better than that, Stacy," Dan scolded her. "That there horse would give his life for you."

"I didn't realize you were such a romantic," Stacy scoffed.

Greg leaned on the upper rail, aimlessly scratching Rio's neck as he looked at her. "Maybe you've been spending too much time in dusty bank vaults and not enough on the back of a horse."

"Bank vaults aren't dusty and Rio is only a horse. Horses aren't capable of that kind of self-sacrificing love and you both know it." It seemed to her that all three males looked at her with identical expressions of accusation. Swallowing a guilty giggle, she silently vowed to make it up to Rio at a later date when it was just the two of them. Now she raised her chin in challenge and looked directly at Greg. "I'm leaving."

"I'll walk you to your car." An iron hand locked on her upper arm.

Stacy went without protest. Away from Dan's curious ears she and Greg could battle out their differences.

CHAPTER FOUR

THE midmorning sun burned the chill from the crispness of the November air. A familiar sound sent Stacy's gaze skywards. Three sandhill cranes, their long legs pointed behind them, were silhouetted against a canvas of blue as they flew south to the wildlife preserve near Monte Vista. Their haunting cries filled her with a restless longing to be as free of the stranglehold of the Valley as were the cranes. What a bizarre notion. Nothing tied her here, while the freedom of the cranes was an illusion. They were bound to the San Luis Valley each spring and autumn by the mysteries of migration and the need for food and shelter. By contrast, the Valley was a place she no longer needed and had left behind. An immense sadness swept unexpectedly over her.

Greg was watching her face. "What's the matter, city girl, can't take the fresh country air any more?"

"I prefer French perfume to barnyard smells."

"If that's what you were wearing this morning when I hauled you out of bed, I prefer it, too." He laughed at the look she gave him. "I appreciate a sweet-smelling woman even if she won't share my bed."

Stacy suddenly felt unprepared to argue that particular subject. "C.B. always got such a kick out of telling everyone how you proved him wrong with Rio."

A small quirk of Greg's mouth told her he recognized the change of subject for the evasion it was. "Rio was no dummy. He quickly figured out it was easier to go

along with me because, in the end, I always get my way."
Greg paused. "Perhaps you've forgotten that."

"I haven't forgotten for one second that you are the
most single-minded, mule-headed person I know." Stacy
stormed over to the porch, startling a small flock of
brown and red house finches into flight. She grabbed
her bags, swinging them away from Greg's reach. "I am
perfectly capable of carrying my own things. Just as I
am perfectly capable of getting my own divorce." Earlier
she'd seen her car and she headed for it.

Greg leaned against the front fender as she opened the
car door and tossed her luggage in back. "Next time you
come, wear the proper clothing," he said.

"There won't be a next time, but you'll be happy to
know my father didn't like my dress last night either.
I'm sure your precious Lucy Fraser will be glad to oblige
both of you by wearing her pink ruffles and bows for
the rest of your lives."

"I was referring to those sissy city clothes you've got
on."

"What's wrong with what I'm wearing?" she flared.

"I'd hate to see you wearing that on the back of a
horse."

"I'm not on the back of a horse, am I? Nor likely to
be. We use automobiles to get around Colorado Springs
these days." She stood with her back to the car, one
hand on the roof, the other holding open the door. "Besides which, your likes and dislikes don't interest me one
tiny bit."

"No?" Greg stepped around the open car door. "Then
I suppose there's no point in mentioning how much I
liked those indecent pajamas you were parading around
in earlier."

Stacy didn't like the provocative innuendo any better than she liked the sexy way Greg had drawled it or the way he was trying to crowd her into the farthest corner of the small triangle formed by the car and the open door. He was entirely too confident he could control her with his size and masculinity. That might have been true once, but no more. She refused to yield one inch of ground to him. "Don't think you can embarrass me with some sort of vague claim that I was trying to seduce you. We both know my pajamas are perfectly respectable. All you could see were my hands, feet and head."

"Respectable? Maybe on somebody else." Greg leaned toward her, bracing himself with one hand on the car door. "On you with those long dance-hall legs?" He shook his head slowly. "Not when I knew damned well you weren't wearing a stitch beneath them." His chest brushed against hers.

"You didn't know any such thing." Out of the corner of her eye Stacy could see Rio watching them intently. A magpie squawked in disdain from the top of a shed.

"I knew." Greg rubbed the collar of her green silk shirt between his fingers. "The button holes are too big for the buttons. The third button down," he circled a button on her shirt with his finger, "had worked itself free."

"A gentleman wouldn't have noticed." A small whirlwind whipped up a dusty plume and the acrid smell of dry weeds floated past her, bringing with it the faintest reminder of Greg's after-shave. She tightened her grip on the car door.

"I'm just a dull country boy, remember?" He slipped his hands under her wool blazer and slid them up to rest on her shoulders. His thumbs traced large circles at the edges of her collarbone. "When I see a woman half out of her pajamas, my mind naturally makes the leap to imagining that woman in my bed."

She swallowed hard, trying to ignore the riot of sensations set off in her stomach by Greg's sensual massage. "If you're apologizing for your offensive behavior this morning, fine."

"A man shouldn't have to apologize for thinking a woman is desirable."

Stacy pressed down hard on the car roof with her left hand. "That isn't what I meant and you know it."

He loosened her death grip on the door and lifted her right hand to his mouth. "I know it." He closed his teeth gently over the fold of skin between her thumb and forefinger. "You taste like apples. No wonder Rio likes to nibble on you."

Stacy caught her breath. Rio's lips brushing her palm didn't send flame stabbing through her veins. "I accept your apology," she said weakly. His mouth was pressed against the pulse at the inside of her wrist. Pressed too hard. He must feel her blood pounding against his lips.

He lifted his head. "What apology?"

Stacy felt giddy. It must be the sudden rush of blood from her wrist. "I——" What were they talking about? Greg encircled her wrist with his hand, his thumb brushing lazily over the surface of her skin. Every tendon, every muscle, every nerve quivered. Removing his hand from inside her jacket, Greg lifted her hand from the roof of the car and on that wrist, too, his thumb worked a mind-fogging magic.

"I used to think you smelled like a meadow after a summer rain when the wildflowers were blooming." He brought her hands behind her back, corralling her body close to his. "Now you smell exotic and mysterious."

He trailed his mouth down the side of her face. "A strange territory I want to explore."

The last lingering remnants of tension fled before soft-spoken words that puffed lightly against her skin. With a sigh Stacy closed her eyes and melted into Greg's embrace. Tiny kisses, like the downy snowflakes of autumn, drifted to the corners of her mouth. Greg explored the rounded curve of cheek and jawbone before moving up to press featherweight kisses against her closed eyelids. When his lips trailed down the side of her face Stacy turned her head searching for his mouth. He caught her bottom lip between his lips and lightly tugged. Sensation shot through her body, startling a low moan from deep within her. His mouth closed over hers as gently as an aspen leaf settling on the ground. His body was warm and strong and she burrowed closer, seeking the comfort he offered. Home, she thought dazedly, where I belong. Protector, lover, friend...

Greg opened his mouth over hers, scattering all thought. He caught her chin between his thumb and finger and gently pulled, parting her lips. His kiss was moist and hot and deep. When he slowly withdrew and straightened up, Stacy felt an aching sense of loss. Slowly she opened her eyes. The sun shone brightly behind Greg's head, turning him into a dark silhouette. The glare hurt her eyes and she wanted to look away. But she dared not. "Why did you do that? Kiss me like that?"

"I told you. You're a desirable woman and I like the way you smell." His hat brim shaded his eyes. "What else?"

Disappointment lay heavily on her chest. "I thought maybe it was in the nature of an apology?" she said carefully. "For tormenting me this morning with your demand that I sleep with you or you'll contest our divorce.''

"Oh, that," Greg said dismissively.

Relief spread through her body, easing taut muscles. "I knew you were being outrageous for the sake of upsetting me."

"Outrageous?" Greg pressed his palm against her cheek. "Maybe so, Slim," he slowly drawled, "but if you want a divorce, you'll meet my condition. I haven't changed my mind. You ought to know me better than that."

Driving out of the Valley toward Poncha Pass, Stacy was still trying to wipe Greg's kiss from her mouth. She was as angry with herself for lowering her barriers as she was with Greg for forcing his stupid kiss on her. A lump, half sob, half laughter rose in her throat. Greg hadn't had to use force. He had even warned her that he expected to get his own way and heaven knew the evidence of his determination littered his ranch. Only a weak, pathetic fool would have succumbed to a kiss that was meant to make her pay for calling him a dull country boy.

His reiteration of her insult should have alerted her that his masculine ego had been dented. Only she wasn't accustomed to thinking of Greg as a man bent on revenge. Revenge was a waste of energy, miring one in yesterday's mud holes, he'd always insisted. Greg should be rushing her to the divorce court, not throwing obstacles in her path. After three years, why had he decided to take his revenge now? Because she'd revealed their marriage to Lucy Fraser? Or because C.B. was dead?

They'd returned from their hasty wedding to discover that C.B. had suffered the first of a long succession of mild heart attacks. The possibility that C.B. might die took precedence over the problem of their marriage. At the hospital, Greg had taken Stacy aside and asked for her silence on the subject of their marriage. He'd wanted to spare his uncle from anything that might distress him and further endanger his health. She'd agreed and that was the last time she'd spoken to Greg until Mary Beth's wedding dance.

C.B. had lived for almost three more years but he'd never completely recovered his health. The time for telling him about the marriage had never been quite right because by then C.B. had made it clear that his deepest wish was for Stacy and Greg to marry. Greg had stalled his uncle with the old excuse of waiting for Stacy to grow up, an excuse C.B. accepted while Stacy finished college and later took the job at the bank in Colorado Springs.

In the three years following the wedding, by faithfully corresponding with C.B., Stacy had managed to keep abreast of Greg's schedule. Thus it was that her visits back to the Valley to see C.B. always "happened" to coincide with Greg's trips away from the Valley. Should C.B. question the coincidence, Stacy had her excuses ready, but the old rancher was obviously too ill to notice anything amiss. Of course she'd seen Greg at his uncle's funeral, but his involvement with his family had given her all the excuse she'd needed to avoid him. For three years their only contact had been the monthly allowance that Greg faithfully deposited in a checking account for her. He'd told her of the arrangement by letter. She'd never touched the money.

A red-tailed hawk took flight from his perch on a telephone pole, his broad wings flapping gracefully as he rose in the sky. Soaring from on high, he'd patiently search the Valley floor for his prey. Such patience was usually rewarded.

Stacy shook off the analogy. She was no scared rabbit for the taking. The adoring child who'd tagged faithfully after Greg, hanging on his every word, convinced of his perfection and infallibility, no longer existed. She'd grown up. Three years of proving she could get along without Gregory Ferris had honed her survival skills. Greg might think he had Stacy beaten, but she wasn't ready to give up yet. It wouldn't be easy but she'd win this battle with Gregory Ferris. She would. She had to.

The doorbell rang as they stood up to leave. Stacy was still laughing at Stan's joke when she swung open the door to her Colorado Springs town house. Her laughter died abruptly. "You."

Greg removed his thumb from the buzzer and straightened up. "Me," he confirmed. He ambled into the town house, checking slightly at the sight of the man standing behind her. Sticking out his hand, he said, "Hi. I'm Greg Ferris. Stacy's husband."

The startling introduction simultaneously imprinted a number of images on Stacy's brain. Stan's face was ludicrous, mouth agape, eyes popping out as he stared in astonishment at Greg. Wry understanding showed in Greg's gray eyes as he lowered his ignored hand. Greg stood relaxed, yet at the same time an air of total masculine satisfaction oozed from every pore in his body. A body which Stacy belatedly realized was draped with a hang-up garment bag. "What are you doing here?" she demanded.

Greg laid his bag over the back of the sofa. "Visiting my wife." Encircling her waist with a long arm, he pulled her up against his firm body. "Miss me, Slim?" He swallowed her denial with his mouth.

By the time she'd fought her way free of an embrace that would have made an octopus proud, Stacy was as flustered as she was furious. It wasn't fair that a man could kiss like that out of sheer orneriness. If she'd seemed to respond for a second or two, it was only because Greg had surprised her. How would she explain to Stan? Not only the kiss, but the husband.

"He's gone." Greg correctly interpreted her involuntary look. "I hope you didn't have hot plans with him tonight."

"Not that it's any of your business, but we were on our way to eat dinner. His wife is out of town." She immediately cursed herself for mentioning Stan's marital status.

"Wife?" Greg raised his right eyebrow a fraction of an inch. "I take it I arrived just in time."

"In time for what? My car wouldn't start, the garage hauled it off, and Stan brought me home. I offered him a drink, he mentioned Nan was out of town and we decided to go out for a bite to eat. Stan works at the bank with me, and I like his wife, so get your mind out of the gutter. And get you and your clothes out of my house," she added in outrage as Greg picked up his bag and headed up the stairs.

"This must be your bedroom," he said, standing in the open doorway. "I'll take the other one."

"You will not."

He turned. "That was easy. You've made up your mind."

Heat rushed to her face as Greg deliberately misinterpreted her remark. "You won't take either bedroom because you're not staying here. I don't know what game you're playing now, Gregory Ferris, but you can go play it somewhere else."

"So you can play games with this Stan?"

"I don't have to explain my actions to you."

"And I don't have to explain mine to you." He disappeared into Stacy's spare bedroom.

"That's what you think." She rushed after him. Greg was hanging clothes in the closet. "What are you doing?"

"Putting my clothes away." He unzipped his bag and pulled out socks and underwear.

"Not in my house you're not."

"Well, not in here," Greg said in mild disgust, shutting the last dresser drawer. "Don't you ever throw anything away?"

"Yes. I'm throwing you away."

Greg laughed. "Being married hasn't dulled the sharp edges of your tongue." He put his underwear back in his bag.

Relief flooded Stacy's body. A short-lived relief. Moving some books to the floor, Greg laid his bag on top of the dresser. "I don't want you here," she said.

"I thought we still had to negotiate an agreement, Slim." He barely glanced her way. "Your mom said you weren't coming home this weekend, so here I am."

"You promised me time to think about it."

"You've got time." He pulled a pair of polished boots from his luggage and set them on the floor. "Knowing you, I thought you might like another opportunity to argue about it."

"Since when has arguing with you ever changed your mind?"

He grinned across the bed at her. "I don't recall that it ever has but I know how you like a good fight."

"A person can't have a good fight with you," Stacy retorted. "You're so damned positive you're always right that words just bounce off your thick hide."

"That's because I know you never mean half the stuff you yell at me." He gathered up his shaving gear. "Where's the bathroom? I was running late so I decided to shower here." He walked around the bed. "I should have taken the time to shave." He touched her cheek lightly with his finger. "You've got a slight case of whisker burn. Sorry. I didn't intend to grab you the second I walked in the door."

"Of course not." She pushed away his finger. "How could you possibly know that you were going to be stricken with an animal urge to mark your territory?" She sniffed. "You've been spending too much time around horses."

"In case you mean that literally, I'm off to the shower." He smiled engagingly at her. "As good as you smell, I hope you have some soap in that shower a man could use."

"Of course I do. What do you think Stan uses?"

The jolted look on Greg's face buoyed Stacy's spirits as she went downstairs. Gregory Ferris was too big to remove physically from her house, but he wasn't going to have things all his way. She supposed he'd get around to telling her in his own good time what he was doing in Colorado Springs on this particular Friday evening. Exactly five and one half days after she'd torn out of his driveway swearing she'd slit her throat before she'd fall into bed with him. Not that she'd had any hope Greg would take her threat seriously. He knew she wasn't the suicidal type. Neither was she the type to submit tamely to Greg's ultimatums. Greg had practically accused her of staying away from the valley this weekend out of cowardice. He was wrong. She hadn't been hiding from him, merely postponing their next encounter. Greg was being amiable now because he thought he had her boxed tightly in. Let him gloat. There had to be a third option open to her. It simply hadn't occurred to her yet.

"Hey, Slim."

Stacy counted slowly to ten. "My name is Stacy."

"I need some towels. This dinky thing wouldn't dry a baby."

It was tempting to ignore him but Greg was capable of walking down the stairs wearing nothing but the towel so that he could show her exactly how little of his body the towel covered. She didn't want to know. Mental pictures of his tall, lean body in her shower, the water cascading down his tanned chest were already giving her fits. She forced herself to remember that sleeping with Greg had not been wonderful. His kisses were pleasant, but anybody could kiss. The sound of the bathroom door opening upstairs galvanized her into action. "I'm coming. Keep your shirt on."

"I don't have a shirt on. That's the problem."

Thankfully the door to the guest bathroom was shut when she walked into the spare bedroom. At her knock, the bathroom door opened to expel a cloud of steam. "Here." She reached around the door and blindly held out a couple of large towels she'd taken from the clothes drier.

"Thanks." Greg grabbed her hand along with the towels. "Better?" He rubbed her palm over his freshly shaved face.

His skin was warm and smooth and slightly damp. The moist air swirled over her, dense and fragrant with musk. "You brought your own soap," she said, almost in accusation.

"I didn't know about Stan."

If the wooden door wasn't between them, she knew she'd see Greg's eyes gleaming with amusement. He'd had time to think and concluded that her words were more challenge than truth. Annoyed at her own transparency, Stacy tugged free her hand. "You still don't," she said crossly.

Greg chuckled. "I will before I go home. Now, be a good girl, Slim, and hand me my clothes from the bed."

If her mouth hadn't suddenly turned to dust, she'd refuse. Greg using her shower, her handling his underwear—the scene was impossibly intimate, too much like real married life. Stacy forced herself to walk toward the bed. Greg would read meaning that didn't exist into a refusal to do something so simple as touching his clothes. She turned, the clothing in her hand.

Greg stood in the bathroom doorway, one of her large towels wrapped loosely around his hips. Stacy's heart skipped a beat. Her imagination hadn't done justice to his sleek body. Several rivulets of water ran through the sprinkling of light brown hairs on his tanned chest. One drop clung to a male nipple that had reacted to the cooler bedroom air by hardening into a small point. Stacy thrust the clothing in Greg's direction. He returned to the bathroom and she flopped down to sit on the bed and closed her eyes. A mistake. Greg's half-naked form was printed on the inside of her eyelids. In full, glorious, living color. She realized that Greg was talking. "What did you say?"

"Where do you want to eat?"

"I don't. Not with you."

Greg reappeared around the partially opened door. "Do you realize this is the first time I've been away from the ranch in over a year? Between C.B. and the chores that got neglected because of his illness..." He pulled a gray sweater over his damp head. "Dan promised he'd call if any emergency came up." Sitting beside her he tugged socks over his long feet. "Even the weatherman has promised no blizzards for a few days."

Suddenly Stacy knew how it had been for Greg the past few years, watching his beloved uncle slowly dying and unable to reverse the course of nature. The uncle who'd been more mother and father to Greg than his own parents had been. Hurting and helpless, Greg would have been cheerful and strong for C.B.'s sake. Once she would have been at Greg's side helping him and C.B. Instead she'd contributed nothing more than cheery letters to C.B. and quick visits to his bedside. Greg had carried his burdens alone. The only thing she was more certain of was that Greg wouldn't welcome her sympathy now. She forced words past a throat clogged with unshed tears. "I'm not cooking."

"Okay." Greg stood up, tamping his feet into his boots. "Did I tell you how much I like your hair that way?" he asked.

"Yes." *Damned sexy,* he'd called it, but she wasn't about to remind him.

"You waited until C.B. died."

The flat statement seemed to require an answer. "You know how C.B. was about long hair being a woman's crowning glory."

"I thought maybe cutting your hair was symbolic. Off with the old. No more Slim. No more long legs in dusty jeans swinging on to the back of a horse. C.B.'s dead and this was your way of bidding *adiós* to the Valley and your past. On with the new Stacy Hamelton. City girl."

She shrugged, uncomfortable with his perspicacity. Even to herself she hadn't admitted all her motives. "I don't have time in the morning for all the fussing long hair requires."

Greg smoothed his hair with the palms of his hands. "You know what I can't decide—are the changes only cosmetic or do they go all the way through?"

Stacy stood up. "All the way through," she said firmly.

"I wonder." Standing in front of her Greg tipped up her chin, and studied her. "Prove it."

The hunk of hair had fallen over his forehead again. Stacy was tempted to yank it out by the roots. "I don't have to prove it," she said. "I grew out of my country-girl phase long ago. This is where I belong now. The only thing you need to wonder about it how despicable you're going to feel after destroying my parents, because I am not about to sleep with you."

A slow smile crinkled the skin around Greg's eyes. "See. I was right." Giving her chin a quick squeeze, he moved away to pick up his dirty jeans. "You do want to fight about it." He transferred the pocket contents to his clean jeans.

Stacy escaped to the doorway. "I don't want to fight——"

"Good." Greg took her arm and escorted her down the stairs. "I don't want to fight either." At the bottom of the staircase, he turned, his solid body blocking Stacy's descent. "Just for this weekend, let's forget our two-hour-long marriage, forget the divorce, forget that three years ago our friendship ran smack into a huge boulder that split us apart and sent us down separate paths." He slid his hand down her arm and played with her fingers, his gaze never leaving hers. "Can we do that,

Slim? For two days, can we turn back the clock and pretend we're the lighthearted friends we used to be?''

"Why?"

His hand tightened momentarily around hers. "Life was easier then, wasn't it? No problems C.B. or your folks couldn't solve. Few responsibilities. It seems like a dream now."

"Your dream," Stacy said tartly. "You peacocking all over the valley while I was relegated to the role of your faithful, adoring servant." There was a perverse pleasure in standing on the bottom step looking down on him. Being taller than Greg seemed to endow her with some sort of magical power over him.

"No wonder I have such a fondness for the past, if you spent all your days at my beck and call, waiting on me and worshiping me." He wove their fingers together. "I have trouble remembering that part." His smile was rueful. "You can spend the weekend refreshing my memory. What say we call a temporary truce? Please."

She was a fool, but she'd never been able to say no to Greg when he stooped to using that humble tone of voice. Even at the age of ten she'd realized he was manipulating her, but she was helpless in the face of warm, melting gray eyes that pleaded with her, at the same time inviting her to be amused at his game. The sense of sharing, of being wrapped in a conspiracy with Greg, had been her downfall every time. Never mind that the conspiracy was actually a conspiracy of one directed against her. Greg was waiting patiently for her answer. As if he didn't already know it, she thought with a sudden spurt of anger.

Greg pressed a finger over her lips. "You started to say yes and then changed your mind," he said quietly. "Why?"

She pulled his hand away from her face. "You're trying to manipulate me and I don't like it. I'm not a child any more."

"I know. I'll show you what the grown-up Stacy does to me." He pressed the palm of her hand against his chest. "Feel my heart racing?"

"No. All I can feel are the thick cables of your sweater." And the heat from his skin. And the pounding of her own pulse.

"You're not trying," Greg said. "Do you think I'd bother to shave for the scrawny kid you used to be? Not to mention polishing my good boots, dousing myself with after-shave and wearing a new sweater that matches my eyes."

In spite of her best resolutions, Stacy felt her lips twitch. "Aren't you afraid of overkill? Besides, the sweater is a lighter gray than your eyes."

"That's your fault," Greg said in a lazy drawl.

"My fault?" Stacy repeated. "I suppose I'm sending out some kind of sexual lure that gets your male hormones all hot to trot and darkens your eyes."

"Actually," Greg said in a neutral voice, his face deliberately without expression, "my eyes get darker when I'm in danger of starving to death."

Sure he was trying to seduce her and intent on the best way to foil his seduction, Greg's remark took Stacy by total surprise and for a long moment she stared nonplussed at him. Then her sense of humor surfaced and she giggled. "Chinese or Italian?"

"Italian."

"Greg." She stood outside her town house door as he locked it behind them. "I let you manipulate me again, didn't I?"

"Don't take it to heart, Slim," he soothed her. "At least you held out longer than you've ever held out before."

"I should have turned around and gone right back into the house," she said again a while later as she handed the menu to the waiter who'd just taken their order. "I don't know why I didn't."

"Don't worry, I promise not to read any significance into your coming. You're a working girl. Why shouldn't you take advantage of a free meal?"

She looked suspiciously across the table. "Because I'm not so sure it's free. How much is it going to cost me?"

"One weekend is all." Greg unleashed his slow smile. "One weekend of riotous city living. One weekend of no chores and sleeping in and reading the morning paper in the morning. One weekend of strolling through the malls instead of loading up at the feed store."

"Uptown women and downtown thrills," Stacy said dryly.

"Exactly."

"You don't need me for that." Stacy reached for her napkin.

Greg covered her hand with his. "It wouldn't be nearly as much fun playing hooky alone."

Stacy gave him a mocking look. "I thought you considered the San Luis Valley to be paradise, the Garden of Eden and heaven all wrapped up into one."

"Even angels travel down to earth once in a while."

"What do angels have to do with you?"

He ignored the gibe. "I love the ranch and I love the Valley. You know that." He rubbed callused finger pads over the back of her hand. "But everyone needs to cut loose once in a while, break free of his responsibilities."

Once again Stacy thought how painfully difficult the past few years must have been for Greg. "How do I know you won't spend the weekend harassing me about sleeping with you?''

"I won't. Scout's honor."

"You weren't a boy scout."

"No, I wasn't." Greg turned over her hand and ran a finger over the tracery of lines in her palm. "I didn't have that kind of childhood. My parents weren't fond of activities for me that might make demands on them."

Stacy retrieved her hand and thrust it in her lap with her other hand, at the same time ruthlessly shoving from her mind the image of a small boy sitting forlornly on the steps of a New York brownstone. "It won't work, Greg."

He gave her a sad smile. "You used to trust me."

"I used to believe in the tooth fairy, too."

"All right."

His was the perfect performance. Hurt feelings plastered over with a quiet dignity. The picture of a man too proud to beg. She wondered how long Greg could sustain the performance. The waiter brought their dinners.

"As soon as we eat, I'll take you home and get my clothes."

"Fine." She picked up her fork.

"It's only a little over three hours' drive back to the ranch. I don't mind driving in the dark. Even if it does snow."

"You said the weatherman promised no snow."

"He did. That's what worries me. You know how weathermen are always a hundred and eighty degrees off."

"Give it up, Greg." She handed him the basket of garlic bread. "It won't work."

"That's a shame." He lifted his glass of wine to her in acknowledgment of her victory. "The new you is someone I'd like to get to know."

Stacy dug thoughtfully into her pasta. The notion appealed to her. Here was the opportunity to prove to Greg that she was no longer the scrawny kid who'd worshiped at his heels. She'd show him that Stacy Hamelton had grown up to be an independent woman who had no need for the likes of Gregory Ferris. "All right," she said abruptly. "Promise me no hanky-panky and you can stay."

"I promise."

The faintest trace of smugness in Greg's voice brought her head sharply up. She immediately recognized the amusement in Greg's eyes. He'd done it again. She knew it and he knew she knew it. "Darn you, Greg Ferris," she said heatedly.

"You're angry." The amusement faded from his eyes. "It used to be our private joke, something special, a game between you and me." He started to reach across the table and then withdrew his hand. "I'm sorry," he said quietly. "I didn't realize you really minded."

Suddenly Stacy didn't mind. It had been special. Greg said that for one weekend he wanted to forget the differences between them. He'd asked for a truce. She put down her fork and held out her hand. "All right. A cease-fire." Her hand was swallowed up by Greg's large hands. Her wrist looked white and sickly compared to his tanned skin. She felt the heat and the calluses and the strength of his hands. "For the weekend."

"For the weekend."

Stacy blinked back tears. It was lucky Greg hadn't thought to use their special game to lure her into his bed. At least, an inner voice whispered, it would be over, a quick way to get her divorce.

CHAPTER FIVE

"COME on, lazybones. Rise and shine."

Stacy opened one eye. Her window was a pale gray rectangle in the darkened room. "It's not even morning." She pulled a blanket up over her head.

"It's ten o'clock." The mattress lurched to one side as Greg sat down. "It's raining."

"Good. On rainy Saturdays I stay in bed."

"If you insist."

The mattress bounced some more. Stacy flipped down her blanket and looked warily at Greg. "What's the big idea?"

His grin bordered on wolfish as he propped his boots on the footboard of her bed. "If that wasn't an invitation——"

"It wasn't. I invited you into my bed once, and once in a lifetime is more than enough for me."

"Since we declared a weekend moratorium on fighting about that subject, I can only surmise that you're a grouch in the mornings." Greg folded a pillow behind his back and settled comfortably in beside her.

Stacy groaned. "Don't you dare be bright and chipper. You're the one who kept me up talking about C.B. until two this morning." At the time of C.B.'s death, their estrangement had prevented Stacy from uttering more than the most conventional, stilted condolences to Greg. Last night had been their private, unofficial wake for C.B. After she'd shed tears, they'd laughed over shared memories. "My eyes feel as if they're glued shut."

"Your eyes and your ears. Your phone has been ringing off the wall since before seven."

Stacy lay on her back, her eyes closed. "What were you doing up at seven?"

"Nasty habit, getting up early. Aren't you going to ask me who called?"

"No." She crossed her hands across her stomach. "I assume Stan spread the word."

"The question is, how is this going to affect your social life? Long-lost husband turning up unexpectedly..." He nudged her leg with his foot. "That was in the nature of a question."

"I'm surprised you didn't ask my callers."

"I wouldn't think of snooping in your private life."

Stacy laughed. "In other words, no one would tell you." It felt good to be back on the old, familiar friendly footing with Greg. He'd been her surrogate older brother. She'd simply confused sisterly affection and romantic love and her stupid behavior had driven away the best friend she'd ever had. Last night gave her hope that Greg was willing to resurrect their friendship.

"I did have a long conversation with Ed," Greg said. "Apparently you two go way back."

Her eyelids popped up. "I don't know any Ed."

"That's not what he said."

"He's lying," she said flatly. "I haven't been out..." She stopped, unwilling to finish the statement.

Greg had no such qualms. "You haven't been out with a man since we were married."

She closed her eyes, refusing to look at him. "It didn't seem honest." The second the words left her mouth she regretted them. "That's not to say it was wrong if you dated, that is...oh, darn." She knew her face was flaming scarlet. "Hoof 'n mouth disease strikes again. The kind of marriage we had . . . I know you'd never lead another woman on. Your wanting a divorce so you can court that schoolteacher is proof of that." She opened her eyes and gave Greg a lopsided smile. "But I don't know any Ed."

"That's strange, Slim, because this guy swears you and he have been having a relationship for over a year, and he sure seemed intimately acquainted with——"

"He's lying." Stacy bolted upright in bed.

"—the inner workings of your car," Greg finished smoothly.

"My car," she repeated blankly. Understanding dawned. "My car!" She grabbed her pillow and pummeled him with it. "Ed is the mechanic at the garage."

"I know that." Laughing, he warded off her blows.

"I know you know that." She redoubled her efforts. "You tricked me into telling you that I haven't dated. Of all the sneaky, low-down coyotes . . ."

"Take it easy, Slim." Greg ducked and the pillow swung harmlessly over his head. "How was I supposed to know you were dying to divulge all your girlish secrets?"

"Girlish secrets! I'll teach you not to be so snoopy." She aimed for his belt buckle.

He grabbed the pillow and a short tug-of-war ensued at the end of which Greg lay on his back, his long arms pinning Stacy on top of him. The battered pillow separated them. "Pax?" he asked in a laughing voice.

"Never." She struggled to free her hands from his iron grip. "There'll be no peace until you abjectly apologize for——"

"For what? Confirming what I already suspected." The laughter disappeared from Greg's voice. "Three years of your life a desert barren of affection and love."

Stacy heard the harsh edge to Greg's words and ceased struggling. "It wasn't that way at all. I had friends."

"Friends. You should have had men falling at your feet."

"I thought our situation was a forbidden subject this weekend." Stacy propped her chin on the pillow between them and looked down at Greg. "However, if you want to discuss any of your recent sexual activity, I'm all ears."

"Your dad's right. You are a mouthy bean pole," Greg said.

"'Sticks and stones,'" Stacy chanted. "When you resort to name calling, I know you're losing the battle."

"Losing, am I?" Greg tossed the pillow to the floor and flipped her on her back. "Ready to give up?"

"Never," she said automatically, wiggling to dislodge him.

"Of course not." Greg shifted his weight to the side, keeping one solid leg over her thighs. "Do you know what your problem is?" he asked conversationally. "You have too damn much pride and you don't know the meaning of the word quit." He threaded his free hand through her hair. "I've seen you dirty and tired and crying from anger and exhaustion. But I've never seen you quit."

Stacy lay still. One of Greg's arms was beneath her, his hand imprisoning hers. The knot of fists protruded into the small of her back but Stacy was scarcely aware of the discomfort. She was too busy trying to ignore Greg's finger tracing the outer rim of her ear. Trying to ignore his mouth scant inches from her lips. He lowered his head, she closed her eyes and then Greg was standing beside the bed, and Stacy didn't know if he'd brushed his lips against hers or if the tingle she'd felt had been nothing more than the fabric of his shirt grazing her mouth.

''I ate breakfast hours ago, but if you get a hustle on I'll whip you up some flapjacks.'' Greg walked out of the room.

Stacy stared at the empty doorway, chilled with the abrupt loss of Greg's body heat. He hadn't kissed her. They'd indulged in a childish tussle and she had expected him to claim a victory kiss. Greg knew she expected it and he'd walked away. Walked away because he wanted her to know exactly what he was offering her. Friendship. Two weeks ago the most she'd hoped to gain from this messy situation was a speedy divorce. Last weekend she'd been positive that Greg wanted nothing more than revenge. His visit this weekend was clearly for the purpose of mending fences. And nothing more. Stacy squeezed her eyes shut. If she weren't so tired she'd leap out of bed and jump for joy.

She pleated the sheet with her fingers. Her revelation that for three years she'd honored their marriage vows had not prompted Greg to make the same claim. The morning he'd dragged her from her bed, at breakfast he admitted that their situation had frustrated him. Had Lucy Fraser helped ease his frustration? Not that it was any of Stacy's business. Even if she was still his wife.

Greg was flipping the last pancake onto her plate when Stacy came down the stairs, showered and dressed for the day. ''Smells good,'' she said brightly.

''The best flapjacks you'll ever eat,'' Greg boasted.

Stacy busied herself with butter and syrup. ''What's your plan for the day, cowboy?''

''Ed first. He has a couple of things he wants to show me on your engine.''

''Why you? It's my car.''

"Ed seemed downright relieved to hear you were married. I had the feeling he's uncomfortable with women like you knowing so much about cars and engines. It wasn't fair not to tell him you grew up on a ranch and were always tinkering with machinery. You walk in his garage looking like a cross between a model and a banker and talk about pistons and rotors and valves and poor ol' Ed's so confused he can't remember which hand holds a screwdriver." Greg wiped off the griddle.

"He didn't tell you that." She cut into her pancakes.

"He didn't have to. Look at you. A shiny white silk blouse and three pounds of silver chains hanging around your neck. A man looks at those long legs in those sassy black pants and he's never going to believe those same legs used to spend hours sticking out from beneath a tractor. You stand there with pale pink fingernails without a chip in the paint and not a hint of dirt. What's the poor guy supposed to think?"

"The same thing he'd think if he saw a man wearing a suit and carrying a briefcase. That I might know about cars and I might not. What I look like and what I'm wearing is irrelevant."

Greg sat down opposite her. "Trust me, Slim. What you look like is hardly irrelevant."

She lifted her fork, syrup dripping from the pancakes. "Is that supposed to be a compliment?"

"If I said yes, you'd get a swelled head. Eat your breakfast. We have a busy day planned."

"No, we don't. I have a day of doing my laundry planned."

"All right." Greg gave her a slow smile. "We'll build a fire in the fireplace, open some wine and listen to the rain falling on the roof." In a lazy drawl, he added, "I'll fold your undies for you."

Greg's words conjured up visions of large tanned hands holding her scraps of lace and dainty silks. "Never mind," she said hastily. "I'll do the laundry after you leave."

"Somehow I thought you would."

Of course he did, Stacy thought later in some annoyance. Greg always knew all the right buttons to push to get her to do exactly what he wanted. A person might be excused for wondering if Stacy had any willpower at all when it came to Gregory Ferris. "Well, I do," she defiantly told her image in the mirror. "Oh, yeah?" her formally dressed twin inelegantly jeered.

Besides, the only reason she'd balked at Greg's plans was to make it clear that he needn't think he could pop up out of the blue and expect her to drop all her plans and be at his disposal. Stacy made a face at her reflection. Doing one's laundry hardly qualified as the type of scintillating activity that would impress Greg but it was unfortunately the best she'd been able to come up with. If the truth were told, she'd been glad she hadn't had other, unbreakable plans. The prospect of spending the day with Greg had dangled before her an unexpected treat.

And it had been a day to treasure as one treasured the small moments of one's life. After they'd conferred with Stacy's mechanic, Greg had suggested a visit to the Fine Arts Center. Stacy wasn't surprised when Greg exhibited a fondness for Charles M. Russell, but his knowledge of *santos* had astonished her until he'd admitted that the grandfather of one of his hands carved the Hispanic religious folk images. Over a late lunch in Old Colorado City Greg had been charmingly attentive, listening with interest to her banking tales. After lunch they'd gallery-hopped their way up and down Colorado Avenue.

Arguing the merits of some of the artists, their wrangling had been good-natured.

Stacy had forgotten how interesting and entertaining Greg could be. He might be a country boy now by choice, but his early upbringing was reflected in his wide-ranging interests and cosmopolitan conversation. Used to seeing Greg in his ranch environment, Stacy had discounted the influence of his parents even though she knew he made frequent visits back east and had traveled to Europe with each of them. As a child, she'd never appreciated that there existed a whole world outside the Valley. Today, planning to impress Greg with her hard-won sophistication, she was disconcerted to discover he was as familiar with adjustable-rate mortgages, amortization, current bestsellers, the latest Broadway hit, Jackson Pollock and wine lists as he was with shoeing a horse.

Her lipstick tube dropped onto her dressing table now. It was hardly surprising that Lucy Fraser had fallen hard for Greg. Stacy wondered what the teacher thought of Greg's visit.

"I don't need anyone's permission to visit my wife," Greg said when Stacy put the question to him over dinner. He leaned back in his chair and studied Stacy over his wineglass. "Is that the kind of wife you'd be, Slim? One who'd hog-tie her husband and never let him out of her sight?"

"What kind of question is that when you've been free as a bird for the past three years?"

Greg sipped his wine, his eyes never leaving her face. "Have I?"

"Of course you have." His stare made her nervous. "I thought we weren't going to talk about our marriage."

"All right. We'll talk about something else. Such as the little black number you're wearing. You look like a nun with those long sleeves and high neckline. Until one realizes there's hardly any bottom to the dress. Two gentlemen across the room about swallowed their forks when you took off your coat. I take it short skirts are back in style." He smiled. "You were a leggy thing as a kid," his voice was fondly reminiscent, "and you're still all legs." His voice subtly altered. "It's funny how legs dressed in black silk look so much different from legs clad in blue denim."

Greg's slow drawl wrapped Stacy in warm comfort. Until she caught the look in his eyes. An intensely raw look, elemental male, full of heat and darkened gray desire. Stacy's world tilted; her heart thudded against her rib cage. It was crazy. Greg didn't feel that way about her. He said something to the waiter and then turned back to her. Familiar gray eyes smiled at her. The warm gray of Topsie's kittens and baby birds. The sudden notion that something precious had been within her grasp and she'd lost it threatened to overwhelm her. Greg was talking to her. Stacy looked blankly at him. "What?"

"I said who would have guessed that a lanky kid who always sprawled all over the floor tripping up the unwary would turn into this." He saluted her with his wineglass. "Although I'm not sure that the raving beauty isn't easier to accept than trying to imagine you with a briefcase."

"You're not trying hard enough." In the past such a flattering remark from Greg about her looks and she would have floated on cloud nine. Tonight she merely acknowledged it with a slight smile. "Our Ms. Hamelton, as they say at the bank, is an up-and-coming financial star."

"You've found your true calling, in fact."

She nodded as the waiter set her dinner in front of her. "In an odd sort of way, I guess I ought to thank you. If I hadn't been running..." Her brain clanged an alarm but she'd already said too much.

"Running?" Greg prompted. "From me?"

"Just running." She took a bite of dinner but Greg was still waiting. "I was scared," she said finally.

Greg's fork clattered to the table. "Of me?" he asked in a tight voice. When Stacy didn't immediately answer, he swore softly. "I hurt you, didn't I? Damn. I was a stupid, drunken fool. In too big a hurry to consider it was your first time." He clenched his fist tightly around the stem of his wine glass. His knuckles shone white under the restaurant lights.

Belatedly Stacy realized that her silence had misled Greg. She reached across the table and touched his hand with the tips of her fingers. "Pooh," she said lightly. "Quit bragging."

"Bragging?" Greg looked at her in disbelief.

"Thinking you're a big, bad cowboy who scared away the little woman. All right, I was scared, but not of you. I messed up and I didn't know what to do. Chicken Little, that's me. I couldn't face my parents or C.B. with the truth and, after the mess I'd landed you in, I was too embarrassed to face you. So I ran. And in running, I found out where I really belong."

"In the city." Greg carefully cut his meat. "It's funny how much a person's house tells about her."

Stacy blinked at the *non sequitur*. "If that's true, yours says you're lazy. Every room in your house looks as if C.B. had just stepped outside for a minute."

"It's a question of conserving energy. A wife will turn the whole house upside down changing it to suit her. Why go through the fuss and bother twice?"

"As I said, pure laziness."

"Maybe so." His gray eyes teased her across the table. "If you moved in there, you'd probably enshrine C.B.'s old Stetson, not to mention that ancient set of elk antlers he had." He gave her a lazy smile as she opened her mouth. "Don't bother to deny it. Hell, you'd probably build a glass case for his last tally book as if it were the family bible."

"I wasn't going to deny it. I was merely going to say that how I'd decorate your house is immaterial. You should be more concerned with Lucy Fraser's taste. I hope you like sleeping with flowered chintz and layers of ruffles."

"I intend to sleep with more than that."

Meaning Lucy Fraser. No doubt with all her feminine wiles and girlish ruffles Greg's schoolteacher knew all the latest ways to please a man in bed. "Your precious Lucy Fraser better not throw away C.B.'s hat," was all Stacy could think to say.

Greg refilled her wineglass. "What gives you any say in the matter?"

The painful awareness that she had none stopped her for a long moment. "You could always give his hat to me."

Greg set down the carafe of wine. "C.B.'s hat'd curl up and die in that sterile place you call home."

"It's not sterile," she indignantly denied. "What do you know about modern décor?"

Greg chewed his meat slowly. "I know what I like and it's not black and white with red cushions looking like slashes of blood on sofas that are harder than frozen sod. There's not a bit of you in that room. That room is a little country girl trying hard to be a big-city sophisticate."

"I'm not trying. I——"

"You still have your old boots. I saw them sticking out from under your bed."

"So? I still ride with Dad occasionally."

"They fit with the rest of your bedroom. The old quilt your great-grandmother made, the faded Indian blanket, the red plaid flannel sheets. I saw the photograph, you know."

She knew instantly what he meant. "It's the only one I have of Rio. I couldn't figure a way to cut you out of it."

"I have one of him alone. I'll give it to you."

"Thank you. I'd appreciate that." Greg didn't answer but applied himself to his dinner. She picked at her food, forcing herself to eat even if the food was shimmering on her plate. Greg would think she was a complete idiot if she broke into tears because he'd offered her a picture of Rio. The photo of Greg with Rio was the only remaining link to her childhood dream. Not that she any longer believed or wanted to believe that dream. It was just... Putting away the photo would be so final. Like death.

The waiter brought coffee and Stacy sipped it gratefully. Around them voices hummed, glasses clinked, plates clattered. The restaurant was small with tables too close together so that the conversations around them ran together. The waiter, in passing, bumped the back of Stacy's chair and murmured an apology. Next to them, two couples laughed at a shared story. The enticing aromas of various entrées did little to tempt her appetite. She fiddled with the handle of her coffee cup.

"Why so sad, city lady?"

She looked across the table. Greg was watching her, his eyes so warm that the past three years almost slid away. She caught herself just in time. This wasn't the Greg of her youth. She forced a smile. "Not sad. Just not hungry. I ate too much at lunch. I hate to waste good food."

Greg studied her a moment longer, clearly not believing her. Then he signaled to the waiter. "Don't worry about it. We can always eat after the concert."

"I'd be a blimp if I spent much time with you," she said a few minutes later, buckling her seat belt.

"That would be a shame." Stacy's coat had fallen open and Greg slid the palm of one hand down her silk-clad thigh to her knee. "I kinda like these just the way they are." He flipped her coat over her legs.

"I never realized what a leg man you are," Stacy said with determined brightness. Her skin felt scorched from his touch, and her mind befuddled. Greg had appeared on her doorstep asking for a truce for the weekend. He'd promised he wouldn't harass her about sleeping with him. And he hadn't. No hints, no sly innuendoes, no hidden messages... At least, no verbal hidden messages. He hadn't kissed her this morning when she'd expected his kiss. On the other hand, if he were anyone but Greg, she'd be wary of little things. The way his hands seemed to linger on her shoulders when he helped her on and off with her coat. The way he touched her at every excuse. The way his gaze focused on her lips while she was talking. She grew hot inside her coat. The night was warm for November.

"Legs like yours, especially in that dress, have a way of intruding on a man's mind. This beat-up old ranch wagon of mine doesn't do them justice. A city gal ought to be chauffeured about in a duded-up car."

"Like the sports car we saw for sale at the garage this morning?" He nodded and Stacy asked, "Why don't you buy it? Your tongue was practically hanging out from the second you saw it. I'll bet you left drool marks all over the red paint."

"It's a car for city slickers, not for a cowpoke like me."

Someone who looked less like a cowpoke at the moment, Stacy couldn't imagine, but she was silent. Greg's inappropriate self-characterization was only one of the evening's peculiarities. Without turning her head Stacy was aware of Greg's large hands casually and competently managing the wheel. His hand hadn't felt casual on her knee. And she didn't think she'd been mistaken about the look in his eyes at dinner. Stacy wished she knew what was going on. One minute Greg was teasing her about being a city girl with just the slightest edge of disparagement in his voice and the next he was blatantly showering her with sensual compliments. Neither of those worried her. It was when Greg purred like a tom cat who'd spotted a dish of cream that he made her nervous.

The large lobby of the Pikes Peak Center was crowded with symphony patrons, many a-glitter with silver, gold and diamonds. Others strolled about sporting turquoise jewelry in every hue of blue green. Well over a century after its founding, Colorado Springs, dubbed "Little London" by an early populace for its many English citizens, prided itself on being a city where the aristocrat and the cowboy freely mingled. Back-slapping and down-at-the-heel cowboy boots were as common as French perfume and designer dresses. Stacy considered the older man greeting Greg with a wide smile and outstretched hand. Wearing shiny cowboy boots and a well-cut suit, the man could be a banker, an airforce colonel or a computer engineer. A second look told her she knew the man.

He was something in politics. And apparently on good terms with Greg.

After exchanging laughing greetings with the man, Greg drew his attention to Stacy. "The way you're eyeing her, I can tell you don't recognize Lloyd Hamelton's daughter, Stacy. Slim, you remember Kurt Lawson, don't you?"

"Stacy Hamelton," the man repeated in astonishment. "Not Lloyd's girl? Lordamighty, gal, the last time I saw you, you were knee-high to a grasshopper." He turned back to Greg. "That explains what you're doing in the city. I know you're allergic to crowds."

"Crowds, yes." Greg wrapped Stacy with a possessive smile. "Beautiful women, no."

Kurt chortled. "No one ever accused you of being stupid." His voice sobered. "Sorry I couldn't make it to C.B.'s funeral. You know I would have come, but I was in Europe. Didn't hear about him passing on until I got back home."

Greg nodded. "Your office called."

Kurt frowned. "It's a shame about the will. I never thought C.B. would do a thing like that to you. Did you know?"

"C.B. told me. It was his to do with as he pleased. You off the leash tonight?"

"Naw, the missus is around here somewhere. Gossiping, I'm sure. Speaking of which, about this will——"

"Didn't I hear your daughter won some scholarship to a school back east?"

Stacy smiled as Kurt Lawson's chest visibly swelled and he expanded on his daughter's triumph. The house lights blinked and, after a few more pleasantries, the politician nodded to Stacy and left in search of his wife.

Stacy took hold of Greg's sleeve. "What was all that about C.B.'s will?"

Greg guided her toward the staircase. "Nothing important. A couple of charity bequests. A few stipulations for disposing of stuff. Some unfinished business he wanted to be certain I took care of." Greg's voice was wooden.

Stacy shot him a quick glance. His face told her nothing but Greg only used that tone of voice when he was hiding his true feelings. If someone like Kurt Lawson saw fit to apologize to Greg for C.B.'s will, that meant C.B. had put something in the will that Greg's friends interpreted as injurious to Greg. Or insulting. Stacy stopped abruptly in the middle of the staircase. "Did C.B.'s mind turn funny?"

Greg nudged her on up the stairs, his hand against the small of her back. "C.B.'s mind was just fine."

"It couldn't have been," she said positively. "If C.B. wanted you to do something for him, all he had to do was tell you. He knew that. Writing it down in his will was the same as saying he didn't trust you to carry out his wishes and C.B. knew better than that. You couldn't be dishonest if you tried. No, C.B. must have been really ill at the end if he didn't trust you."

The door to the box was in front of them. Greg turned her to face him, his eyes intent on her face. "That sounds rather funny coming from you."

Stacy reached up and straightened Greg's red tie. What she'd thought were elongated Paisleys turned out to be stylized pheasants. "In spite of how things might have looked at times," she traced a pheasant with her finger, "I always trusted you. It might not have seemed that way, but that night I wasn't scared of you. I admit I was frightened by what we were going to do, but not because of you. I trusted you. Even..."

"When you hated me?"

"Oh, Greg," she raised troubled eyes to his face. "I never hated you." His face was sceptical. "Yes, well, I suppose I did," she said with a rush of honesty. "You were so angry because I'd messed up everything and it was easier to be furious with you than to admit it was all my fault. I felt so guilty and I didn't know how to make it up to you and so, well, everything got tangled up in my mind, but I never didn't trust you. I mean, you'll laugh at me, but a couple of times, when things seemed particularly grim in my life for one reason or another, I would tell myself that if things got worse I could go to you and you'd help me. Even after you'd said what you said, I thought, I mean I really knew, that I could trust you and that——"

"Dammit, Slim, how can you blurt out that idiotic, juvenile nonsense now?" Grabbing her elbows, he pulled her close, his eyes glinting with anger. "When are you going to grow up?"

"I am——"

"The hell you are. You might have a grown-up job and dress like a grown-up, and, dammit, look like a grown-up, but you're nothing but a damned baby." His fingers slid above her elbows and tightened. "I want you to look at me. Really look at me. I'm not a saint. I'm a man with flaws and pimples and warts, and you're too old to indulge in hero worship."

"If you're trying——"

"I'm trying to force you to grow up and open your eyes. It used to scare the hell out of C.B. the way you worshiped me. Because he knew me. I'm not perfect. I've got a fault that's a whopper and you've always refused to see it. I'm single-minded. When I want some-thing, I go after it until I get it. Nothing or no one is allowed to stand in my way.'' He gave her a sharp shake. ''Listen to me, Slim. No one. Not even you. If I want something and you're in my way, I'll run right over you.''

Her arms ached. ''I don't believe you.''

''Dammit, Slim, believe me. I won't want to, but I will. No matter how I hurt you. Because that's the way I am. I'm not some goddamned paragon you've dreamed up.''

''Why are you saying these things to me?''

''I don't want you coming around whining later,'' Greg said evenly. He slid his hands up to her shoulders. ''Consider yourself warned.''

Stacy stared blankly at Greg. For him to threaten her... The anger in Greg's eyes dissolved and reformed into a wry amusement. The frozen block of ice inside Stacy thawed slightly. She must have imagined the threat. ''A man who is aware of his faults can change,'' she said.

Greg slipped a hand inside the collar of her coat. ''I don't want to change.''

CHAPTER SIX

GREG'S soft-spoken words hung in the air. His hand was warm against Stacy's neck. Uncertainty flooded over her.

The door to the box opened. "Greg." A tanned, male face peered out. "I thought I heard your voice out here."

Greg greeted his friend, introduced Stacy and ushered her into the box. Another man stood up, two women turned and a flurry of introductions followed. Down on the stage the orchestra warmed up, the inharmonious notes a suitable accompaniment to Stacy's chaotic thoughts as her mind raced frantically in circles seeking to decipher Greg's cryptic remarks. The houselights dimmed and the audience burst into applause as the conductor strode onto the brilliantly lit stage. The symphony orchestra. A man like Greg should have tickets to an evening of cowboy poetry. A man like Greg. He probably did enjoy cowboy poetry as much as classical music. She was discovering this weekend how little she really knew him.

Musical waves of sound beat against Stacy's temples. Bach, Irving Berlin or the Beatles, she hardly cared. Greg sat beside her, a wool-clad arm brushing against her when he applauded. The scent of his after-shave wafted past her nose and she stirred uneasily. Greg wanted something and he was warning her not to stand in his way. There could be only one thing that Greg wanted that had anything to do with Stacy. A divorce so that he could marry Lucy Fraser. Which made no sense. She'd offered to set him free. Insisted, in fact. Greg was the one

101

throwing up obstacles. The one who refused to seek a divorce until she slept with him.

Stacy's throat ached with unshed tears. She'd taunted Greg with the sordid failure of their sole sexual experience. Now he intended to salvage his male pride by proving to her that she could find pleasure in his arms. Once she'd capitulated to his lovemaking, then he would divorce her. Greg was right. She was foolishly blind. He hadn't been able to force her into his bed, so he'd come to Colorado Springs to seduce her in hers.

How cleverly he'd cast his lures. Last night he'd established the bond between them with nostalgic tales of their past. This morning his failure to kiss her had convinced her he wanted nothing more from her than friendship. One minute lightheartedly teasing her, the next bestowing lavish compliments with sensuous overtones, Greg had kept her off balance all day. If seduction was indeed his goal, he must be feeling quite confident of success. How unfortunate for him that her lamentable sense of timing and foolish babbling about trusting him had provoked the very protective instincts he insisted he didn't possess. It was ironic, but Stacy wasn't misled. The fact that Greg warned her didn't mean he wasn't perfectly capable of carrying out his intention. Obliged by good manners to sit and smile and converse all the while wanting to jump up and scream with hurt made Stacy's head ache and chafed raw her temper.

Sleet was spitting from the sky when the concert goers poured from the Pikes Peak Center. The ice-glazed pavements glittered dangerously beneath Stacy's feet as they hurried to the car. In the car, the slick streets and heavy traffic required all Greg's concentration. Across from the well-lit Palmer Center the statue of two men on horses caught Stacy's eye. The statue had always reminded her of Greg. Too much reminded her of him. It was time to consign Gregory Ferris to the past. Once and for all. Starting just as soon as they safely reached her town house.

Greg beat her into speech. "You've been quiet tonight. Didn't you enjoy the concert?"

Jerking away, she thwarted his attempt to help her off with her coat. "How could I be expected to even listen to a concert after what you said?"

"Forget what I said."

"You call me names and threaten me and I'm supposed to forget it?" Her voice was pitched too high. Greg would equate hysteria with immaturity. Stacy swallowed hard, struggling for control. "Your stay with me is over." She hung up her coat, closing the closet door in Greg's face when he reached for a hanger. "Go home. I don't want you here any more."

Greg tossed his coat over the back of the sofa. "I think we ought to talk." Strolling out to her kitchen, he opened cupboard doors. "How about a cup of coffee?"

"I don't want to talk and I don't want a cup of coffee. What do you think you're doing?" She scowled at him from the kitchen doorway.

"Fixing coffee." Greg measured a spoonful of instant coffee granules into a mug and filled the mug with water. "I've never known anyone who can bear a grudge longer than you."

"Bear a grudge!" Stacy gasped. "You can accuse me of that when you're the one who——"

"Remember that time," he interrupted, "when a pheasant spooked Scarlet and she dumped you in a mud puddle and I laughed?" He stuck the mug in the microwave.

"I'm in no mood to reminisce," Stacy snapped.

"It took you a month but you finally managed to dump me in a stock pond in retaliation."

"One of my few pleasant memories of our past acquaintance." She sipped the coffee Greg handed her.

He lolled against the cabinet, as much at ease in her small kitchen as he was on the back of a horse. "Over the years, we've built up a whole storehouse of memories, mostly good ones."

"I assume there's some point to your rehashing history."

"There is." He took a second mug of coffee from the microwave. "Why are we letting a couple of sour memories wipe out all the good ones?"

"Maybe my memories aren't as good as yours."

"And maybe you're too stubborn to see what's right in front of your nose."

"The only thing right in front of my nose is you and you're leaving. Just as soon as you finish your coffee," she added in a lame attempt to save face. Greg would leave when he felt like it and, short of calling the police, they both knew there wasn't a darned thing she could do about it.

Greg took a long swallow of coffee. "I've been giving this divorce some thought and I'm not so sure we ought to rush into it without thinking the matter through."

"It's hardly rushing when I've thought of little else for three years," Stacy said.

"You thought about divorce, or you thought about our hasty, furtive marriage and the reason for it?" Greg asked bluntly.

Stacy felt her cheeks flame with heated color. "What difference does it make?"

"It makes a difference. If, for example, you want a divorce because Prince Charming is waiting in the wings."

"I don't believe in fairy tales anymore," she said bitterly.

"You're too young to be so cynical."

"Stop accusing me of being a child. I admit I was immature three years ago but I've done a lot of growing up since then."

Greg set down his mug and moved across the room to where she stood. "A hell of a lot," he agreed. He took her mug from nerveless fingers and set it on the counter top. "I wasn't sure I even knew you any more."

Stacy walked into the living room, putting distance between them. "You don't need to know me to divorce me."

"Are you sure you want a divorce?"

"Of course I'm sure." Stacy swung to face him. "I suppose that's your convoluted way of asking if I want a divorce badly enough to sleep with you. I should have known from the minute you showed up that your little surprise visit was more than a sudden urge for a vacation." She dropped to the sofa, clutching a cushion to her middle, anger churning her insides. "Did you think a sneak attack would prevail where threats failed?"

"I wasn't completely honest about the reasons for my visit," Greg said slowly, "but it's not what you think." He sat in her black leather chair, his legs sprawled across her rug. "When you're standing at the corral feeding Rio an apple, all I see is the same Slim I've always seen, maybe a little fancier dressed, a little taller, a little older, but basically, no different."

"I'm not——"

He went on as if she hadn't spoken. "I wanted to see you on your turf, away from the Valley. I wanted to find out for myself how deep the cosmetic changes went."

"All the way through."

"No. You spend too much time trying to prove you don't belong in the Valley any more." A faint smile curved his lips. "Like wearing fancy clothes at the ranch."

"I'm not protesting too much."

Greg didn't bother to argue. "Since I haven't changed——"

"At last we can agree on something. You're still as opinionated and arrogant as you always were."

"And you're still as quick to rush heedlessly into battle."

"I'm not rushing into divorce," Stacy said. "You know darned well you want this divorce as badly as I do."

"I know that for thirteen years we had a very special friendship. Then, in one night of folly, we blasted that friendship into smithereens." Greg stood up and walked over to the window, brushing aside the curtains to stare into the wet black night. "A lot of water has passed under the bridge since then and what we once had is lost forever." After a pause, he added, "I'm not even interested in searching for it."

"Then why bring it up?" People mourned dead friends. They didn't mourn dead friendships. Pain swept over Stacy. Greg's coat lay beside her on the sofa. His scent lingered on the wool.

"Because I think we can build something new." He moved to stand in front of her. "We can stay married, become friends again." He looked steadily down at her. "Only different friends this time. Friends as equals."

The idea was as appealing as it was astonishing. "I have my job," she said weakly. It was the wrong response. She tried again. "It's impossible."

Greg sat down, freeing the cushion from her rigid hold and tossing it to one side. "I'm not insisting that you move to the ranch. Keep your job if you like." He took her hands in his. "I'd like you to think about it. The advantages——"

"There are no advantages." His hands were too large. She felt trapped.

"Sure there are," Greg said easily. "Imagine how thrilled your parents are now and how upset they'd be over a divorce."

It didn't take much imagination. Her father and mother had told her over the phone at least a million times how happy they were, each time brushing away her claim that her marriage was a horrendous mistake. "I can't live my life for my parents."

"Your parents' happiness is merely an added bonus. Along with financial security for you——"

"I don't need your money. I'm doing just fine on my own."

He released one of her hands; the other he turned palm down, measuring it against his own large, work-roughened hand. "There's the ranch for weekends and vacations——"

"I already go to my parents' ranch for those."

"You could ride Rio instead of sneaking him apples."

She blinked away the tears stinging her eyelids. "I can't stay married because of a horse."

"I'm merely trying to show you the whole package."

"You've left something out. You."

"Am I such a big obstacle? We managed okay this weekend."

She shot him an incredulous look. "You come waltzing in here without notice and expect me to drop everything I'm doing or planning and entertain you. Is that your idea of managing okay? You always getting your way?"

Greg's hand tightened around hers for an instant. "Suppose I'd called you on the phone and suggested that we try and make our marriage work. What would your reaction have been?"

"That you're totally insane." She finally succeeded in twisting her hand free and she sprang up from the sofa. "And nothing you've said here tonight makes me think any differently. You and I really married. It's so hysterically funny that——"

"Why aren't you laughing?"

The quiet question sliced through Stacy's angry torrent of words. She stood in front of her cold fireplace, tracing the rim of a plate which stood on the mantel. "Because if I do, I'll burst into tears," she whispered.

"C.B. always said you were too honest for your own good." Greg crossed the room and gripped her arms. "Stay married to me and you'd never have to worry about shocking your husband by what you did. You'd be free to speak your mind."

"You didn't mention love." She held her arms stiffly at her sides, every muscle in her body resisting his siren song.

He kneaded her taut shoulders, his thumbs tracing the edges of her collarbone. "Our marriage would be like a pair of comfortable old boots that never pinched."

He was too honest to lie and tell her he loved her. His proposal was impossible. And dangerously seductive. Her heart raced. A beautiful dream that logic warned her was beyond her reach. Greg's gaze was so intent on her face that for a moment she feared he could read the thoughts ricocheting through her brain. Panicked, she spoke the first coherent thought to cross her mind. "You said you wanted children."

"Have you any objections to motherhood?"

"Of course not." He was befuddling her. Decisions were easier when Greg didn't stand so close.

"Your eyes have always reminded me of cotton floating from the cottonwood trees in the spring, bits of white against a blue sky." He leaned closer. "Maybe lots of people have white flecks in their eyes, but yours seem to stand out."

Stacy shook her head, fighting his intense, persuasive voice. "You're changing the subject," she said breathlessly.

"We're talking about our children." His mouth was solemn but, even half concealed under lowered lids as he looked at her, his gray eyes danced with subtle amusement. "Naturally their mother's appearance is of some concern to me."

"Not to me." Greg's face was tanned from working outdoors, his cheeks roughened by the wind. Tiny lines fanned out from the corners of his eyes. "Your children will probably be ornery brats with gray eyes."

"Do you have anything against gray eyes?"

"Yes." They made her go all warm and squishy inside. She couldn't admit that. Sliding away from lips brushing the side of her neck, she crossed to the electric switches and flooded the room with light. "What about your schoolteacher?"

"You said she was wrong for me." Greg leaned against the fireplace, one elbow resting on the mantel.

"When have you paid attention to anything I've said?"

"I'm paying attention now."

"You're not paying attention," she said in a shaken voice, "you're trying to seduce me."

"What if I am? If I'm successful, that answers the question as to whether you find me repulsive after having spent one disastrous night with me."

"Is that what this is all about?" Pain turned quickly to fury. "A stupid macho plan to prove what a man you are?"

Greg could move fast when he wanted to. "I don't need to prove anything to you." He caught her elbows, holding her securely in front of him. "It was an honest proposition. Are you going to consider it like the adult you keep insisting you are, or are you going to act like a baby and cry for the moon?" His mouth softened as he looked down at her. "I can't give you the moon."

Confusion flooded over Stacy. Greg's mouth couldn't possibly be as soft and warm as it looked. And as inviting. Stacy rose to her toes, clutching Greg's shirtfront for balance, and closed her teeth tentatively over his bottom lip. When Greg remained motionless, she grew bolder, tracing the outline of his lips with her tongue and then turning her head back and forth ever so slightly, brushing her mouth against his. The barest flick of her tongue parted his lips.

The rush of pleasure came from a startling sense of coming home. Greg made no move to gather her close, his hands resting quiescently on her shoulders. His restraint was as liberating as it was exhilarating. And reassuring. He seemed to want her to know she could trust him. Heat from his body spanned the inches between them. His suit jacket was wool, his shirt silky fine cotton. Stacy wondered how the contrasting fabrics would feel drawn slowly across the tips of her breasts. Heat surged through her body at the notion, and startled, she drew back and looked wide-eyed at him. The room seemed charged with mysterious currents that swirled around them.

Greg's face was impassive. He touched her cheek lightly with his forefinger. "I'd better head back to the ranch."

Stacy dropped numbly into the black chair, listening to Greg's footsteps ascend the staircase. The ceiling creaked as he moved around overhead. He was whistling. He'd never been able to carry a tune. Desperately she tried to fill her mind with all the times she'd jeered at him for singing or whistling off key. Anything to keep angry bewilderment at bay. Gregory Ferris was the most infuriating and sadistic individual she knew. He'd played her like a fish all weekend, and when she'd finally risen to the bait he'd tossed her back in the river.

"Thanks for putting me up and for putting up with me," Greg said, his garment bag slung over his shoulder. When Stacy failed to respond, his gaze sharpened, locking on her stormy countenance. The silence stretched between them as he studied her thoughtfully. "Don't be an idiot," he said softly.

"Your warning comes too late. I've already been an idiot."

"You wouldn't thank me for agreeing with you."

She gave him an inimical look. "You needn't rub it in."

"I can't help it if you've added one and one and come up with three."

"Quit talking in puzzles. You give me a headache."

"That's nothing to what you give me." A small smile played around Greg's mouth. "Are you mad at yourself for kissing me, mad at me for not kissing you back or mad at me for calling a halt before things got out of hand?''

"If I'm angry, it's at myself for allowing you to manipulate me again. That nonsense about us staying married was a trick to prove how irresistible you are.''

"Am I irresistible?'' he drawled.

"Definitely not. If you're thinking about that dumb kiss... I merely forgot for a minute what a low-down, underhanded snake you are. I think it was your aftershave,'' she added desperately.

"I'll take a bath in it next time,'' Greg promised gravely.

"There won't be a next time.''

"Think about my proposal and let me know.''

"What proposal?''

His smile was crooked. "It's probably a little late to call it a marriage proposal, but that's what it is, all the same.''

Stacy's eyes rounded. "You mean you were serious?''

"Did you think I wasn't?''

"Then why are you leaving?''

"I think it's the black stockings,'' he said, slowly and deliberately scanning her body.

"The black...?'' Masculine heat seemed to leap the chasm between them and Stacy felt her cheeks turn crimson as his meaning sunk in. She curled her legs beneath her in the chair.

"Definitely the black stockings.'' The lazy smile curling the corners of Greg's mouth failed to extinguish the gleam of male appreciation in his eyes. "If I stayed, I wouldn't sleep alone.''

"You wouldn't sleep with me.''

His smile deepened. "I doubt I'd sleep at all.''

Stacy felt suddenly beleaguered by six feet three inches of lazy masculinity. Sitting while Greg stood gave him the advantage and she jumped to her feet. "Go home."

"I am. Come lock up behind me."

"Don't treat me like a child." She opened the front door.

"Don't act like one." Greg wrapped a hand around the nape of her neck and pulled her close. "Take care of yourself, Mrs. Ferris." His mouth closed over hers in a brief but solid kiss. "Take your time thinking about my proposal. Then call me."

"I don't need to think about it," she said when Greg released her. "The whole idea is stupid." He waved from the parking area, a lift of the hand which said he wasn't ready to accept her answer. Sleet was no longer falling, but a hazy fog clung to the plains and the lights of the city glowed eerily. Stacy started to call Greg back but caught herself in time. Fog was common in the San Luis Valley. He would have no trouble driving in it. She slowly closed her front door, securely locking it. Greg was gone but the feel and taste of his lips against hers lingered on.

The sensations resurfaced at odd moments during the following week as Stacy waged internal debate. Had Greg been serious or not? He'd been pretty vague about why he didn't want a divorce. As for the reasons he'd glibly listed meant to dissuade her from getting a divorce, they were ludicrous. Her parents and Rio? And he must know she didn't need his money. So why was he proposing they stay married? What was in it for him? His side-stepping the question of love was as good as a flat statement saying he didn't love Stacy. He even admitted he wasn't interested in resurrecting their past friendship. What did he really want from her? Children? Lucy Fraser was doubtless at the head of a long line of women who would be thrilled to bear Gregory Ferris's children. It hadn't escaped Stacy that Greg had evaded answering several key questions, starting with the one named Lucy Fraser.

Greg's motives and Lucy Fraser aside, how did Stacy herself feel about Greg's proposal? Ambivalent was the best answer she could muster. Over the past three years she'd made a new life for herself. A life that didn't include Gregory Ferris. She loved her job. She loved living in Colorado Springs. All right, maybe sometimes she did miss coyotes howling at night. Maybe sometimes the crazy traffic on Academy Boulevard did give her a horrendous headache. And maybe there were times the surrounding buildings suffocated her until she felt she'd give her last dollar to look out of the window and see a vast horizon stretching before her populated by nothing but cattle. Even Greg had to admit that city life had it all over country life when it came to shopping, or night life, or restaurants, or cultural events or—or running to the convenience store for a carton of milk. If there were times when she missed the country—and, no matter what Greg thought, she was adult enough to admit there were—then all she had to do was visit her parents.

For all Greg's talk, she noticed he had embraced urban amenities with the enthusiasm of a thirsty man finding an oasis. Proving, perhaps, that it was as easy to escape occasionally to the city as it was to escape to the country. If one wanted to do so. Which she didn't. Did she?

Which led her back to the question of Greg. His idea was total nonsense. Two people didn't stay married simply because they were already married and a divorce was too much trouble. So why was she wasting her time even considering the matter? It wasn't as if she still loved him or anything foolish like that. His proposal was nothing more than a puzzle to be solved. Greg never did anything without a reason. Speculation about that reason kept her awake nights. Not even to herself was Stacy willing to admit that she was trying to read more into Greg's proposal than was there. By Friday afternoon, she was no closer to solving her mystery than she was to arriving at an answer for Greg. Turning him down should be easy, and yet...once, long ago, her friendship with Greg had been special.

Stacy didn't see the man crossing the marble bank floor until he called her name. "Mr. Craddock," she said, pleasantly surprised to see someone from back home. "What are you doing here?"

"I was up in Denver pleading a case in front of the Colorado supreme court," the lawyer said. "We finished early so I thought I'd stop on my way home." He followed Stacy to her desk and took the visitor's chair. "I know Greg said he'd tell you, but I thought you might have some questions."

"About what?" Stacy asked, her mind racing. Had Greg changed his mind and approached his lawyer about a divorce without even telling her?

"C.B.'s will, of course," Mr. Craddock said.

"C.B.'s will?" Stacy echoed blankly. "What about it?"

The lawyer told her.

Her car tore along the country road, an angry dust cloud in its wake. A coyote trotting along the ditch beside the road slunk hastily into some tall weeds as the car flashed past. Stacy took the corner too fast. Her wheels skidding on the gravel, she fought for control. The squealing sound of tortured tires startled the kestrel on a fence post into flight. She eased up her foot on the accelerator. Obliging Gregory Ferris by dying was not in her plans. Although when she finished with him, he'd wish he were dead. Of all the dirty, low-down, rotten skunks... An angry tear seared a path down her cheek. How dared he try to pull a fast one on her like that? She didn't care if the ranch was his whole life. By the time she finished with him, he'd wish he'd never left New York City at the age of fourteen.

Gregory Ferris thought he was so clever. Clever! He was a cheating, underhanded, conniving bastard. Now she knew the real reason he didn't want a divorce. To think she'd almost fallen for his slick line of double-talk. Swallowing all that gibberish about friendship and eyes like floating cotton against a blue sky. If she never wore black stockings again... Sniffing, Stacy dashed away another burning tear with the back of her hand. After last night her tear ducts should have closed down from exhaustion. She would have come the second she finished at work yesterday but she couldn't stop crying. Not that she was crying because she wanted to stay married to Gregory Ferris. She rubbed an eye with her knuckles. Being deceived and lied to on such an outrageously enormous scale would make a stone statue cry.

Midway between Greg's house and the barn Stacy slammed her foot on the brake pedal. Ignoring the cloud of dust settling around the car, she leaned all her weight on the steering wheel. Greg erupted from the barn. He was shouting but his words were drowned by the strident blaring of her car horn.

Greg yanked the car door open. "Stop making that damned racket." He reached in and grabbed her hands away from the wheel. "What the hell do you think you're doing?" Gripping her tightly around her wrists, he attempted to pull her from the car.

Stacy stiffened, pushing down with her feet, wedging herself behind the wheel. "Let go of me!"

"Why? So you can scare the hell out of all my animals?"

"Your animals! Why, you lying creep!" Leaning away from him, she tugged with all her strength.

Greg squeezed her wrists tighter. "What is the matter with you? Have you gone loco?"

"Loco! Is that your next plan? Claiming I'm crazy?" Struggling furiously, she threw her body sideways in an effort to retrieve her hands from Greg's crushing grip. "You dirty—rotten—cheating—snake..." Panting from her exertions, Stacy twisted until she was half lying across the seat and kicked outward with her feet.

"Ouch! You wildcat. Stop kicking or I'll——"

"You'll what? You thieving..." She aimed another kick.

Greg dropped on her like a sack of grain. "I warned you," he said as she gasped.

"Yes—damn you—you warned me." She gulped for air. "You wanted—something and I—was in your way." Angry tears threatened and she blinked hard, still struggling to breathe. "You said you—didn't care if you—hurt me."

"I cared."

"The hell you did, you double-dealing bastard. Stay married to me, you said. Let's not get divorced, you said. But it's what you didn't say, you slimy coyote, that mattered." She freed one arm and jabbed her elbow hard in his side. "When were you going to mention that C.B. left part of his ranch to me?"

Greg recaptured her flailing arm and held both her hands above her head. "Les called me this morning. I tried to call you but you'd already left. I can explain if you'll just stop acting like a hysterical maniac.''

"You couldn't explain if you took the rest of your life because, believe me," she said through gritted teeth, laboring to dislodge him from on top her, "the rest of your life won't be very long. I'm going to strangle you with my bare hands."

Greg shifted his weight, sliding his body to the outer edge of the car seat and scrunching her up against the seat back. A muscular leg across her thighs held her lower body immobile while his bent arm rested heavily across her chest. His nose was inches from hers. "You've been crying."

"Damn you, I have allergies."

"Since when?"

"Since yesterday when Les Craddock told me about C.B.'s will. I'm allergic to cheaters, hypocrites——" Greg's mouth cut her off. When he lifted his head, she kept right on going "—swindlers and liars. And if you kiss me once more, Gregory Ferris, I'll break your nose again." She heaved upward with her body. Greg was too strong for her. "Get off me."

"If I do, will you listen to me?"

"Listen to more lies? Not on your life!"

"In that case, I'm quite comfortable where I am."

Stacy turned her head just in time. Greg's kiss landed on her ear. Hardly a victory for her as he sucked on the outer shell before trailing his tongue along the inner whorls. "I'm going to kill you," she snarled into his shirt front. The laughter she felt rumbling deep in his chest stoked her fury and rekindled her efforts to eject him.

Greg closed his teeth over the outer shell of her ear. "Hold still and you'll be fine," he said in her ear. His grip slackened, the pressure across her legs easing. "Are you ready to listen?"

Stacy sniffed loudly. "You're hurting me." She turned her face to him, moisture welling up in her eyes. Two huge drops of water clung to the rim of her eyes before spilling over. More tears followed until her cheeks were awash with salt water.

With a muttered curse, Greg released her and backed out of the car. He held his hand out to her. "Come out of there so we can discuss this like reasonable people."

Stacy shot upright, knocked Greg's hand out of the way and slammed shut her car door, locking it securely. She rolled the car window down a few inches. "We have nothing to discuss, you sneaky, double-dealing, underhanded baboon. That was a filthy trick, threatening me with dire consequences to my parents if I sought a divorce without your permission. Promising me you'd give me a divorce if I slept with you. That must have seemed pretty safe since you knew damned good and well I'd never sleep with you. When did you start worrying that I'd go to any extreme to get rid of a cretin like you? The last thing you wanted was a divorce, because to get one you have to disclose your assets or risk committing perjury. And then I'd have found out the truth about exactly what it is you own and don't own."

She audibly ground her teeth. "You thought you were so damned clever, pretending you wanted to marry me. Friends!" She spat the detestable word at him. "I'd rather be friends with a grizzly bear. Did you really think that staying married to me would keep me from finding out?" Her eyes narrowed. "No," she said slowly, the awful truth hitting her. "You thought it wouldn't matter to me. That you could seduce me into being as besotted with you now as I was as a child. That I'd permit godlike

Gregory Ferris to do whatever he wanted with my property. You were wrong," she said, firmly enunciating each word.

Greg stood beside the car, his arms crossed across his chest, his face expressionless. "Are you through ranting and raving and ready to listen?"

"You're the one who needs to listen, because I'm going to tell you exactly what I intend to do." Stacy bared her teeth in an ugly parody of a smile. "I'm going to sell my part of the ranch. All forty percent of it."

"You can't."

"You're mistaken." The knowledge that retribution was near lent a malevolently complacent tone to her voice. "I can and I will."

"Not without offering to sell it to me first."

"I know," she purred. "C.B. was even kind enough to set down in his will how much you have to pay me for the privilege of becoming sole owner of the ranch."

"You and Les must have had quite a conversation," Greg said coldly.

"Quite." The heady sense of power almost compensated for the manner in which Greg had sinned against her. Almost. She traced the rim of the steering wheel with her right hand, peering up at Greg from under lowered lashes. "It seems you have lots of land and very little ready cash." She blinked her lashes rapidly at Greg and smiled maliciously. "Les said it was lucky we were married because if I ever decided to sell to you it seems you'll have to sell off a good bit of the ranch just to raise the money to buy me out. Isn't that a shame?"

"It would be. If I had any intention of doing so." Greg disappeared around the back of Stacy's car.

She craned her neck to see out the back window. Greg was squatting in the dust behind her car. Stacy heard an ominous hissing sound. "Gregory Ferris, you stop that!" Greg moved around to the other side. Stacy unlocked the door and leaped from the car. The second rear tire settled flatly in the dust with a soft sigh. Stacy screamed with rage and leaped on Greg's shoulders as he leaned down to her right front wheel.

Fending off her fists, he released the valve on the tire and stood up, Stacy clinging to his back like a burr. "Just remember who declared this war," he said.

"You did," she panted, "when you lied and——"

"I never lied to you." He wasn't even breathing heavily as he moved to the next tyre, dragging Stacy with him.

"I'm going to kill you," she said, pummeling his shoulders.

Greg swiftly turned and captured her flailing arms. Pulling her in his wake, he walked around the open car door, reached in, grabbed the keys and slammed shut the door. He released Stacy. "Now, we'll talk."

Stacy took one look at the rigid look on Greg's face and backed away. "There's nothing to talk about."

"A mouthy city girl like you always has her lips flapping." He tracked her relentlessly. "You say you own forty percent of this ranch——"

"I don't say it. I do own it."

"Nobody owns anything until probate is settled."

Stacy wasn't misled by Greg's level tone. He was furious. She quickened her backward pace, seething at his hypocritical anger. By what right did he play the injured party? She was the one who'd been deceived. "Don't split hairs with me. C.B. left me forty percent of this ranch and you know it."

Greg reached out and caught the lapels of her woolen blazer jacket. Before she could wiggle out of the jacket, he hauled her up against his hard body. "All right," he said in a deceptively mild voice. "Since you're a forty-percent owner of the ranch, Mrs. Ferris, why the hell am I doing one hundred percent of the work?"

Stacy squealed as Greg tossed her over his shoulder. "Put me down."

"I intend to, Mrs. Ferris. I intend to." Greg strode across the open ranch yard to the barn and dumped her in a pile of hay.

"Why, you..." Stacy's voice died away as she looked up.

Greg stood looking down at her, his long denim-clad legs spread apart, his fists jammed against his hips, an implacable look on his face. "Now, Mrs. Ferris, since you're part owner of this spread, you can get up off your fancy little city behind and get to work."

CHAPTER SEVEN

STACY curled her fingers around clumps of hay, wariness mingling with disbelief as she absorbed Greg's words and noted his looming stance. The barn was dark and shadowy. Behind her a large animal moved restlessly. A calico cat moved stealthily past and pounced silently. A tiny scream was cut abruptly off. The cat trotted off, something dark hanging from his mouth. A chill clutched at Stacy's spine, a chill she resolutely ignored. She was no timid mouse. "You can't terrorize me into changing my mind about selling, Gregory Ferris. I'm not afraid of you just because you happen to be bigger than me."

"No?" Greg took a step toward her.

Stacy scooted rapidly backward, propelling herself on hands and heels. "No." Annoyed with herself for displaying even a hint of fear, she spoke sharply. "I only came to tell you my intentions. Unlike you, who's behaved like the scum of the earth, I play fair. Now you know where I stand and I'm leaving."

"How?"

She ignored the hand Greg held down to her. "I'll drive one of your cars."

Greg folded his arms. "I don't think so."

On her feet, Stacy brushed away the wisps and bits of straw clinging to her pants. "My mother will pick me up."

"I doubt it. If I know your mother, and I do, she'll tell you you're a grown woman and you have to work this out yourself."

"Not when I tell her you're abusing me and holding me prisoner."

"Sissy," Greg taunted softly. "City living has softened you. You can't even fight your own battles any more. Go ahead. Call up Mama and tell her that her little baby girl needs her diapers changed. Crawl to the phone and beg for help." His eyes mocked her. "Begging for help is one thing you excel at."

The gibe was meant to hurt. Pain slashed across Stacy's middle and she felt the blood drain from her face. "I'll stay the weekend," she said in a stiff voice, "but I intend to be back at the bank on Monday morning. And if you so much as touch me," she added as Greg took a step in her direction, "I'll..." Her frantic gaze found a pitchfork leaning against a stall. "You'll be sorry."

Greg's gaze followed hers. "I'd be a millionaire if I had a dollar for every time you warned me I'd be sorry." He twisted his lips in a wry imitation of a smile. "The truth is, I'm already sorry. Damned sorry."

Stacy gave him an uncertain look. It sounded as if Greg was finally coming to his senses and prepared to be reasonable. Despite the fact that he deserved lynching, she decided to be magnanimous. "I accept your apology. We'll forget this whole episode took place." She took a step toward the barn door.

Greg blocked her path. "Where do you think you're going?"

"Home. You apologized and I accepted your apology."

"I didn't apologize."

"You did. You said you were sorry."

"I'm sorry all right. Sorry I let you buffalo me that night. I'd have been a hell of a lot less sorry these past three years if, instead of sleeping with you, I'd paddled the daylights out of you. At least," he added in a slow drawl, "one of us might have enjoyed that."

Stacy stiffened in outrage. "No doubt you would have. Violence is the only kind of interaction between a man and a woman that a Neanderthal thug can appreciate. You belong here on a ranch with all the other animals. Civilization is wasted on a brute like you." Fury lent her a full head of steam. "A woman with polished finger-nails and educated conversation scares the hell out of you. You prefer silly nitwits who think you're some kind of rawhide god. Well, you're not a god." She jabbed a finger in his chest. "You're nothing but a crude cowboy who can't meet a woman on equal terms. All you're capable of is grabbing and grunting and threatening. I've had it with your juvenile posturing. Call me all the names you want. You're the one who was lying and playing stupid games. And do you want to know the best joke of all?" She stepped back so she could watch his face. "Now I'm part owner and I'm going to make your life miserable," she said with relish, "until you raise the cash to buy me out." With her last triumphant parting words, she stepped around him.

Greg grabbed her arm. "Saddle up Cindy."

"What?" Expecting threats or at least excuses in his defense, the directive threw her off stride.

"I'm expecting someone any minute to ride Cindy. Since you're the reason I'm behind schedule, you can saddle her up. Use the small saddle behind you."

"You didn't listen to a word I said. I'm leaving."

"I heard you. You said you were staying the weekend to help out. And you said that I'd better not touch you." His fingers tightened around her upper left arm. "Since you didn't mean the first, I can only assume you didn't mean the second."

"I meant it." She tried to peel his fingers away.

"You meant which one?" Effortlessly he corralled her right hand in his large hand.

"You know which one." She forced herself to stop struggling. That would be playing right into Greg's trap. "I'm not going to fight you," she said with quiet dignity. "I'm not going to give you an excuse to manhandle me."

Greg laughed softly. "You've already given me all the excuse I need. As long as you intend to make me sorry for touching you," he slid his hand down her left arm and captured her hand, "I might as well make sure the crime fits the punishment." Pulling her arms around behind her, he caught her hands firmly in his, the action pushing her up against his hard body. His free hand cupped the curve of her cheek and then he wove his long fingers through her hair, forcing her to look up into his face.

Ignoring the quiver deep in her stomach, Stacy eyed him belligerently. "You're only proving my point." Her heavy cardigan hung open and his large belt buckle gouged her through her thin cotton turtleneck sweater. "Grabbing and threatening is all you know."

Greg rubbed their combined hands along her spine below the small of her back, pinning her hips snugly against his. He lowered his head. "Do you feel threatened?"

His mouth was mere inches from hers. Stacy closed her eyes. "I'm not afraid of you." Bold words when she was weaker than a newborn calf.

"Good. Because us crude cowpokes like our women tough and feisty. Makes breaking 'em more fun."

Her eyes popped open at the laughter in Greg's voice. The amusement in his eyes told her he was only teasing her. "You make me so mad," she said weakly.

"Since you're already mad, I have nothing to lose if I do this, have I?"

She had no chance to ask what "this' was. Greg's mouth was smooth and possessive and addictive. His body was hard and firm and inflexible. It must be hers that softened and yielded so that they fitted together like two halves of a whole. She'd run the gamut of emotions since yesterday and now she was wrung dry and her body treacherously sought comfort in the enemy's embrace. The enemy. Wrenching her mouth from Greg's, Stacy overbalanced and stumbled against him.

The sudden movement took Greg by surprise. He stepped incautiously backward, caught his heel on a loose floorboard and tumbled to the floor, twisting his body so that he landed under Stacy. "Are you okay?" he asked.

She nodded weakly, her face burning with embarrassment, her gaze firmly riveted to his top shirt button. "Are you?"

"Are you kidding? I'm lying on a soft bed of hay with a long-legged beauty sprawled across my chest." His long arms locked around Stacy. "You can't leave now. Not in the middle of what was turning out to be a downright interesting——" he rolled them over, pinning her beneath him "—conversation."

His canvas shirt was a faded black. "We weren't talking." The pulse at the base of his neck throbbed, sending waves of warm scent over her. Stacy felt a ridiculous impulse to press her lips against the tanned skin in the open V of his shirt.

Greg propped his upper body on one elbow. "I could have sworn you were saying something." Picking up a length of straw, he tapped the tip of her nose. "I'm just not sure what."

"In spite of your caveman tendencies," Stacy chose her words carefully, "sometimes kissing you can be rather enjoyable." Feeling his eyes on her, she turned her head. A mistake. Her only view was the corded muscles of Greg's bare arm below his rolled-up shirt-sleeves.

"In spite of your shrewish tendencies," Greg mimicked her voice, "sometimes kissing you can be rather breathtaking."

A hand on her chin positioned her mouth beneath his. She would have protested had Greg allowed her to do so. Her indignant gaze told him so. Or would have. If she hadn't shut her eyes to block out the strange smoldering intensity in his. The sounds and odors of the barn faded away as Stacy surrendered to the exquisite pleasures evoked by Greg's hands and lips. Her body felt like rising bread dough with his knowing hands kneading and shaping her pliable softness. Companionship and comfort, the twin pillars of friendship, Stacy thought. Lying in Greg's embrace felt as right as it felt good. Burrowing deeper into his chest, she tightened her arms around his neck and returned his kisses unstintingly as his fingers stroked, his tongue explored and his mouth possessed. Sensation piled upon sensation and pleasure became need.

Greg raised his head. "If I'd known settling this was as easy as tackling you in the barn, I'd have done it long ago."

Stacy went very still. "What exactly is it we've settled?"

Greg dropped an easy kiss on her parted lips. "What we talked about last week. Staying married."

"I see. You still think that's a good idea," Stacy said. Greg gave her a slow smile that reeked of male complacency. He seemed totally unaware that one of his hands was resting on her right breast, his thumb curled around a tip that hardened in spite of her firmest resolve. "May I get up?"

Greg's eyes narrowed at the coolly polite request but he rolled to one side and rose lithely to his feet. "Let me help you up." His voice matched hers. "If you're going to pick another fight," he looked down to where she still sprawled on the scattered hay, "I think we're both safer if you're standing."

Stacy considered ignoring the hand he extended down to her, but the look in his eyes warned her against it. She allowed him to pull her to her feet. "You're the one who drew up the battle lines when you tried to trick me into staying married to you just because I happen to own something you want."

Greg leaned against a nearby stall, shredding a piece of straw with his long fingers. "And in revenge for my so-called trick, you kissed me."

Her cheeks flamed but she refused to back down. "The fact that I enjoy being kissed by a man, any man," she stressed, "is immaterial to this discussion. You own sixty percent of this ranch. I own forty percent. I'm going to sell my share. If you want to buy it, you have to come up with the cash."

"And our marriage?"

"I'll file for divorce this week. Now that I know why you were throwing up your ridiculous obstacle——"

"The condition stands," Greg said coolly. "Sleep with me or I'll fight the divorce."

"I don't think you will. Because the tables are turned." She didn't try to keep the triumph from her voice. "Oppose the divorce and I'll tell the whole world not only why you're fighting me, but how you tried to cheat me. You told Les you'd tell me about C.B.'s will." She snapped her fingers. "So much for your reputation as an honest man."

Greg tossed the straw bits to the floor. "You can threaten to paint me as black as you want but that doesn't give you the edge you seem to think it does." He swung down a small saddle from a nearby stall and walked out of the barn.

Stacy hurried after him. "What do you mean?"

Greg gave an affectionate slap to the small mare standing patiently inside the corral. "Say what you want about me. I don't care. The question is," he smoothed a colorful horse blanket over the mare's back, "will you care if your folks are upset if I start spreading interesting little titbits about you? We both know you'd never deliberately hurt them."

An angry haze dimmed Stacy's vision. She was so furious that it was a few minutes before she could trust herself to speak. "You think you've won, don't you?"

"It's not a matter of winning or losing." Greg tied Cindy to the corral top rail. "By right, the ranch belongs to me."

"Well, I don't think so!"

Resting his forearms on the small saddle, Greg studied her over the mare's back. "You don't know where you belong."

"How very cryptic," she mocked. "And very wrong. I belong in the city and I'm going back there. Right this minute."

Greg cocked an eyebrow. "I thought we'd thoroughly covered that subject."

"If you think I'm staying here after..." Stacy's angry voice died away as a small blue car cautiously entered the ranch yard. Lucy Fraser waved gaily from the driver's seat.

"We'll continue this conversation later." Greg walked toward the car as the two inhabitants spilled out.

For the first time Stacy was aware of the small boy accompanying the schoolteacher. A boy who walked with a limp and was missing part of one arm. Stacy's mother had told her of the car accident that had crippled the eight-year-old. What was the boy doing here with Lucy Fraser? Stacy stayed by the corral.

Greg entered the corral, the boy limping at his side. Untying Cindy, Greg led her into the center of the corral, then he squatted in the dust to talk to the boy.

"You wouldn't believe what coming out here has done for Toby's self-esteem," Lucy said softly at Stacy's side. "He totally withdrew from life after his accident. I read about this kind of therapy and approached Greg about helping. Of course, he immediately agreed."

"How kind of him." And how smart. Win the boy, win his teacher, Stacy thought, watching Greg with the boy. Toby obviously worshiped Greg. And why not? Hadn't she when she was eight years old? Greg's teeth flashed white as he laughed at something the boy said. Stacy smelled the schoolteacher's perfume as Lucy stood beside her. She glanced over. The teacher was intent on what was happening in the corral. The pink ruffled dress had given way to designer jeans and a flowery chintz blouse. The gray ribbon that corralled her curls was the exact shade of Greg's eyes.

Lucy turned and caught the inspection. "I suppose you think I was a fool, going on about Greg the way I did at Mary Beth's wedding."

"I really haven't thought about it," Stacy said stiffly. Lucy was no bigger fool than Stacy.

"Are you that sure of yourself? You don't even bother to wear a wedding ring." Lucy turned her gaze back toward the corral. "I probably ought to warn you," her voice was matter-of-fact, "that I don't consider an absentee wife much of an obstacle."

Taken aback by the woman's candid remark, the best Stacy could manage was an inanity. "Is that so?"

"I don't know why Greg has tolerated the situation as long as he has, but I have reason to believe his patience is running out."

Stacy refused to ask for clarification of the provocative remark. Greg's behavior was underhanded and deceitful in the matter of C.B.'s will and the ranch, but Stacy refused to believe that he'd discuss his marriage and divorce with Lucy. No matter what the other woman thought she knew, Stacy was positive Lucy's knowledge didn't come from Greg. At least, she was pretty sure it didn't. Who was she to know what men talked about when they shared a pillow with a pretty woman? And Greg had never denied sharing a pillow with his precious schoolteacher.

After a long moment, Lucy started chatting about inconsequentials, her impressions of Colorado, her students, the weather. Stacy mumbled answers from time to time, her mind busy with the implications of the teacher's first remarks. Gradually the pair in the corral captured her attention. Toby was afraid of the horse. Placid, easygoing Cindy wouldn't hurt a fly but she must have seemed enormous to the boy. Greg was patient, never rushing the boy and making it clear that Toby didn't have to do anything he didn't want to do. Greg's quiet belief in Toby gave the boy courage and soon Toby was bouncing awkwardly around the corral on Cindy's back, Greg jogging alongside shouting words of encouragement. At the end of an hour, Stacy was as drained as if she'd been the one forcing the boundaries of her courage.

"They're marvelous, aren't they?" Lucy said softly. "Not once has Greg shown Toby the slightest hint of pity." She wiped her eyes. "This is the first time Toby has ridden alone. He said last week he wanted to but I could tell on the way out here today that he was terrified. I almost said something to Greg, but then I realized I could trust him not to give Toby more than he was ready for." She raised her voice. "Hey, cowpokes! You about done riding the range for the day? This here tenderfoot is getting mighty thirsty for a sarsaparilla back in town."

Stacy stood mute. She'd believed the teacher was using the boy to get closer to Greg. Lucy's last remarks had shown her in a totally different light, compassionate and caring and wise enough to keep Toby from feeling pitied. Here, obviously, was the woman who attracted Greg.

Toby stood on a stump rubbing down Cindy. Not that the mare had worked up much of a sweat, but Stacy knew Greg's aim was to develop a bond between the boy and the horse. Greg's booming laugh echoed Toby's giggles as Cindy blew gustily down the front of the boy's shirt. It was evident that Greg saw beyond the boy's handicaps and admired him for his spirit and courage. When Greg had first moved to Colorado he'd been totally raw and ignorant in the ways of ranching and the west, but he'd had a determination and iron will that had brought him far. He and Toby were kindred spirits. Darn Gregory Ferris for having a good side.

Stacy watched the blue car disappear down the road. "I should have asked her for a ride."

Greg opened the gate to the near pasture and slapped Cindy on the rump. The small mare scampered toward a small herd of horses grazing on the far side. "Afraid she'd say no, Slim? Or did you think that because I'm sap enough to waste time with some scaredy-cat cripple I'd back down and give you your way?"

Stacy had seen too much in the corral to be deceived for one second by Greg's sneering words. Not that she had any intention of letting Greg know that. "I didn't want the boy to be upset by your brawling. He'll find out soon enough that you're an underhanded horse thief."

Greg laughed. "You must find your sense of fair play mighty inconvenient at times. You knew I wouldn't say a word if you left with Lucy. You'd have won our argument by default, only you never could do anything underhand just because it gave you the advantage." He grinned down at her. "It's your bad luck, Slim, that I don't play by the same rules." Sticking two fingers in his mouth, he gave a shrill whistle. Across the pasture, a horse started trotting toward them. The rest of the small herd followed. Greg lifted a coiled rope from a corral post.

"If you think I'm shaking in my boots, I'm not."

"Boots." Greg looked down at her feet. "Those silly things are worthless."

Stacy held up a foot shod in red suede. "I'll have you know they cost me a small fortune."

"You were cheated." A circle of rope floated through the air and landed neatly around a brown gelding's neck.

Even as she admired Greg's skill, Stacy said, "I was not cheated. You don't know a thing about women's clothes."

"I know you can't ride in those boots." He snagged the rope on the corral post. "Come on."

"I'm not coming anywhere and I'm not riding. I told you. I'm going home."

Thirty minutes later Stacy leaned down and patted Quanah's spotted neck. "I know I look strange wearing C.B.'s boots over three pair of socks, not to mention wearing his jeans and old hat, but in spite of that, I'm not taking any more nonsense from you. I don't want to be here any more than you do. Even if you did manage to unload me, Greg would just make me get back on."

Greg reined in beside her. "Not bad for a city girl. For a minute there, when those magpies took off, I thought sure Quanah was going to dust your pants for you."

She gave him an unfriendly look. "You were hoping."

"Now, Slim," he drawled, "it's a gorgeous afternoon. If you were honest, you'd admit you'd rather be on the back of a good horse than stuck in city traffic."

She scowled at him. "What would you know about honesty?" Greg stood up in his stirrups and grabbed her saddle horn, forcing Quanah closer to his gelding. Leaning over, he planted a swift, hard kiss on Stacy's lips. Before she could react, he'd released Quanah and reined his horse to the side. "Why did you do that?" she asked.

Greg grinned at her. "Another woman might have lied. You changed the subject."

"I lie when I want." Unwilling to debate the point, she rushed ahead. "Did you kidnap me to prove you're stronger than me, or is there a point to this exercise?"

"We're going to move about twenty head of cattle from this pasture to nearer the house. As for the point of it..." He made a small sound and the brown gelding picked up speed and circled around a small knot of cattle.

Stacy watched Greg go with a jaundiced eye. One of the hands could have helped him gather these cows. The fact that Greg was patient and understanding with Toby didn't alter the fact that he'd tried to trick her into staying married to him for his own selfish reasons. Impatiently she brushed away a fly. All the kisses in the world, no matter how pleasurable, didn't change that. Gregory Ferris was a selfish, greedy, conniving, mangy creep who thought he could manipulate her with sweet kisses and sugary words. And just what he hoped to accomplish by forcing her to stay this weekend...

She could have left, but she'd be darned if she'd back down in the face of a challenge from Gregory Ferris. Besides, he was right about one thing. It was a gorgeous day for a ride. Snow frosted the surrounding mountains, but the air down in the Valley was warm. Across the creek half a dozen pronghorn antelope skittishly grazed. A century ago bison would have grazed where the cattle were now. Long before C.B.'s ancestors had settled in the Valley, the Spanish had come from the south and before them successions of Indian tribes had made their homes in the Valley before vanishing like the morning mist. If she ignored the telephone poles and the drone of an airliner overhead, Stacy could almost see the Utes, known for their skilled horsemanship, sweeping down Poncha Pass en route to a hunt.

Quanah swerved and took off across the pasture. He'd seen the cow break from the small herd and dash for freedom even if Stacy hadn't been paying attention. For the next couple of hours there was no time for idle day-dreaming or making revengeful plans. Stacy had moved cattle so many times over the years she thought she could do it in her sleep. If she'd grown a little rusty, Quanah was a born cutting horse who turned on a dime and seemed to know where a cow was going before the cow knew herself. Stacy begrudgingly approved of Greg's choice of horse for her as she forced another recalcitrant cow back into the small herd she was trailing through the opened gate. Greg closed the heavy gate behind her.

Back at the corral Stacy slid off Quanah. "Well?" she demanded of Greg. At least he could admit her riding skills hadn't suffered, transplanted to the city or not.

Greg swung to the ground. "I'll flip you. Heads you cook dinner and I take care of the horses." He picked the quarter out of the dirt. "Heads. There's a couple of steaks thawing in the refrigerator."

So much for expecting any praise. "A couple?" She handed him Quanah's reins. "Expecting someone for dinner?"

"You." A lazy grin covered his face. "I told you Les called this morning. I knew you'd be down to raise hell with me."

Stacy gave him a cool look. "I haven't even begun to raise hell yet." She turned toward the house.

Greg reached out and stopped her. "As for your question, you're still the best horsewoman I know, even rigged out like that. You're a lot skinnier than C.B. That belt could go around you twice. All the same," he slowly inspected her from head to toe, "you look damned sexy in his old flannel shirt and jeans."

Some people will say anything to keep a ranch, Stacy told herself, lighting the grill in the oven. Gregory Ferris knew darned well that she knew his only interest in her was her share of the ranch, and he still had the nerve to try and seduce her. Just because he thought he was God's gift to women with his lean six-foot-plus body, wide shoulders and slim hips... Today's woman required more than an aggressively male chin and smoky gray eyes. All right, she conceded, maybe a few brainless women believed everything they saw at the movies and thought cowboys were romantic heroes. She set two potatoes in the microwave. If they only knew the truth.

The scheme burst into her brain with the dazzling excitement of a Fourth of July fireworks display. A dude ranch. Giggling over the lettuce, Stacy worked out her plans.

She fired the first salvo over perfectly cooked steaks. "I've been thinking about this will of C.B.'s and I've figured out a way that we both get what we want."

Greg laid down his steak knife. "Do you even know what you want?"

She ignored the question. "We'll turn the ranch into a dude ranch."

"Don't be an idiot."

She pretended surprise. "You don't like the idea?"

"I don't know what bee you've got in your bonnet now, Slim, but it's not going to work."

"I want to sell my share of the ranch and you want to buy it. The only way you could possibly raise the money is to sell off part of the land and that rather defeats the purpose, don't you think?" Stacy concentrated on cutting her meat. "On the other hand, if you were to turn the ranch into a dude ranch, the money would roll in and you could buy me out in no time."

"As attractive as that notion is," Greg said dryly, "I doubt a dude ranch would be as lucrative as you think. I know a few ranchers who've tried it and failed."

"Don't be so modest. You have an asset they don't have."

"That look on your face tells me I'm going to be sorry I'm asking. What asset?"

"You. The quintessential cowboy. Hordes of women from back east would be thrilled at paying outrageous

prices to spend a couple of weeks or more trailing ador-
ingly behind you.'' She gave him a wide-eyed look, sup-
pressing the laughter that threatened to expose her.

"If this is your idea of a joke, it's a bad one," Greg
said tightly.

This promised to be even better than she'd hoped. Greg
was steaming almost as much as her baked potato. "It's
no joke," she said with just the right touch of earn-
estness. "You're the epitome of the western hero. Tall,
handsome, lean. Your broken nose adds masculine
ruggedness." Stacy shivered ostentatiously. "Sex appeal.
You'd be selling more than a few days roping cattle.
You'd be selling a woman's dream. Of course," her voice
turned practical as she dug into her potato, "you'd have
to practice up on your roping, fancy up your tack with
a heavily carved leather saddle and some silver stirrups."
She eyed him critically across the table. "It's a darned
shame you can't carry a tune. Maybe you can hire a
singing cowboy."

"I could always lip sync," he said coldly.

Stacy pretended to take him at his word. "Too
awkward, carrying a tape recorder on a horse." She
pursed her lips thoughtfully. "What about sequins on
your shirts—or would you rather have silk?"

Greg leaned back in his chair. "No silk, no sequins,
no singing and no dude ranch."

"Are you saying you don't want my share of the
ranch?"

"I want it and I'll get it. Another way. My way."

"You already tried your way." Stacy gave him a patronizing smile. "And failed."

Greg pushed back his chair and stood up. "I don't
give up that easily—Mrs. Ferris." He strode from the
room.

Stacy stuck her elbows on the table and propped her chin on her hands. She knew a threat when she heard one. In a way, she couldn't blame Greg for fighting for what was rightfully his. Since she'd discovered C.B. had left her a share of the ranch, she'd mulled over the reason why and had come to an inescapable conclusion. C.B. had wanted Stacy and Greg to marry and he knew that Greg would court and wed the devil himself if that was what it took to get the ranch. C.B., C.B., Stacy silently admonished. You can't force Greg to love me. Not even for the ranch. A reluctant grin lingered on her face. Leave it to C.B. to make sure that if Stacy and Greg didn't marry, at least Greg could buy back Stacy's portion of the ranch. Obviously C.B. had believed that a pretty remote possibility considering the consequences of such a sale.

Or else the cagey old wolf knew Stacy a heck of a lot better than his nephew did. Stacy had no intention of forcing Greg to sell off part of the ranch. He'd earned the ranch through long hours of back-breaking work. That didn't mean she wasn't going to make Gregory Ferris rue the day he'd tried to play his dirty tricks on her. When he was properly penitent and groveling at her feet, she would give him back his ranch. Then and only then. In the meanwhile—Stacy cleared up the supper dishes and started the dishwasher—she'd only just begun her revenge.

A good night's sleep would prepare her for tomorrow's skirmish. She collected what she could from the kitchen. Upstairs in the bathroom she set her makeshift beauty aids beside the sink. The light had been on in C.B.'s office. No doubt Greg erroneously believed a closed office door was some kind of barrier. He was going to be surprised when she didn't fuss about spending the night on the ranch, but she wasn't through with him yet. Not by a long shot. With a loud, satisfying click, she locked the door connecting the bathroom with Greg's bedroom. He was the one who'd flexed his muscles and insisted she spend the weekend here. He could use the other bathroom. She hung an old flannel nightshirt of C.B.'s on a hook and stepped into the steaming bathtub and closed her eyes.

"I hesitate to ask, but are those tea bags on your eyes?"

Startled into sitting up, Stacy grabbed and missed as the tea bags fell into the bath water. At the same instant she realized that the bubbles from the liquid soap had receded to an embarrassing degree. Ducking under the water, she rapidly churning up more bubbles with her hands. "What are you doing in here?" Stupid question. Greg's door to the bathroom had been locked, so he'd gone through her bedroom. "Go away."

He stepped closer. "Is that plastic wrap on your head?"

Stacy gave him a dirty look. "You seem to have forgotten that I'm being held here against my will because you disabled my car. I had planned to return to Colorado Springs tonight, therefore I did not bring a suitcase. No suitcase. No makeup supplies. Now, if you're through interrogating me..."

"I'm not." He sat down on the edge of the tub. "It is plastic wrap. What's that on your face?"

"If you must know, I'm conditioning my hair in mayonnaise because the wind today dried it out. I have petroleum jelly on my face moisturizing it and the tea bags are for easing stress. And they don't work worth a darn when they're lying on the bottom of the bathtub and you're sitting on the edge of it."

"Why? Do I make you nervous?"

"I don't know what your daily habits are, but mine don't include bathing with a man looking on."

Greg leaned down and swished his hand through the water. "I'm glad to hear that."

"I'm glad you're glad," she said tartly, much too aware of Greg's hand. "Now if you would kindly get out of here?"

"It's my bathroom."

"It's forty percent mine and I'm claiming the bathtub."

"Does that mean everything else is mine. Such as this?" Greg held her bath towel up in the air.

"Put that down."

"Come and get it. Or..." he waved the towel above her head "...we could work out a trade."

"I don't trade with cheating scum."

"Too bad." Greg opened the cupboard and swept all the towels into his arms. Turning, he grinned down at her. "Want to reconsider your answer?"

"No, but we both know I will, don't we? What kind of trade did you have in mind?" She found the tea bags and squeezed them tightly under water, wishing they were Greg's neck. "A towel for one night in your bed?"

"Tempting," his grin grew diabolical, "but as much as I hate to disappoint you, I was thinking more along the lines of a towel for forty percent of this ranch."

Stacy stared in angry disbelief. She'd expected him to demand a kiss. "Damn you, Gregory Ferris," she said at last. "There is no limit to the depths you'll sink to, is there?"

His grin never faltered. "Apparently not. Well? Is it a deal?"

CHAPTER EIGHT

STACY stood up. Her gaze steady on Greg, she stepped from the tub. "No deal," she said in a firm voice. "You can keep your darned towels." Chin high in the air, she marched dripping from the room, snatching C.B.'s nightshirt from the hook on the door as she passed. The stunned look on Greg's face was priceless. And hopefully worth the fact that she'd just acted like a total idiot. When was she going to quit letting Gregory Ferris get under her skin? Her sopping wet, goose-pimpled skin.

"You have to be the stubbornest woman I know." Greg followed her into the bedroom and draped an enormous bathtowel over her shoulders.

Stacy grabbed the ends from him and fashioned the towel into a sarong. "I don't exactly hold the patent on stubbornness around here." She doubted her blush would ever go away but she was darned if she'd defend her actions.

"That's something you ought to remember more often." Greg parked his long-limbed body on her bed, half sitting against the headboard, his hands behind his head. "In case your memory has failed you, I've won far more battles of will between us than you have."

Stacy gave him a saccharine smile. "We all have our own way of remembering history, don't we? Fortunately," she began unwrapping the plastic wrap from her hair, "we're on the same side in this struggle."

"Which struggle?" Greg crossed his booted feet.

"The one to make me a wealthy woman and to save you your ranch. I'm talking about turning the ranch into a dude ranch. We'll have to redecorate," she shouted from the bathroom. The sound of running water drowned out any reply. Greg hadn't moved when she returned to the bedroom, a towel wrapped turban-style around her head. "This room has a certain ambiance that will work, but you'll have to change to another bedroom. Sharing a bathroom with one of your female guests might be construed as her receiving unfair advantage." Stacy vigorously toweled her hair. "On the other hand, we could charge more for this room."

"You forget I'm a married man." His eyes were shut, the lashes dark against tanned skin.

"How can you worry about a detail like that when we've more important things to consider? I was thinking, now that Dan's and Agnes's kids are gone, Agnes has those three extra bedrooms. I'll bet she'd be thrilled to take in guests to earn a little extra money. Agnes could do the cooking, too, if you hire someone from town to help."

"You're just full of ideas, aren't you, Mrs. Ferris?"

"You haven't heard anything yet, Mr. Ferris. I think we ought to name all the bedrooms. Numbers are so institutional." She watched Greg in the mirror. "With all these pictures of kittens and puppies, we could call this room 'Innocence.'"

"I have a better idea. Considering the virulent shade of pink on the walls, call the room the Kitten Crib."

"What a wonderful idea. The ladies will love the idea of staying in a room with such a naughty connotation. Of course, we'll probably have to explain that in the Old West cribs were mini houses of ill repute. How's this for a super idea?'' She swiveled around on the dressing table stool, ''We'll name all the rooms for famous ladies of the night. Pearl de Vere from Cripple Creek and Mattie Silks from Denver and Silverheels, the dance-hall girl who nursed the miners in Buckskin Joe. I'll do some research on it.'' She surveyed him thoughtfully. ''I was wrong about the sequined shirts. The gambling man look suits you better. Black western suit and vest. String tie. As tall as you are, you'll knock the ladies dead.'' She turned back to the mirror and parted her hair. ''Naturally, you won't be able to actually work the ranch; you'd get your clothes filthy. Most of the cows will have to go, but we'll keep a few for authenticity and atmosphere.'' She frowned. ''It's a shame you don't smoke. A cheroot would be the perfect touch. Maybe you could just swagger around with it clenched in your teeth. I can see it now.'' Dramatically she clutched the comb to her chest. ''Legions of middle-aged ladies swooning at your feet.'' The mirror reflected Greg's calm face. Darn him. He wasn't even beginning to twitch. He should be having apoplexy. ''Are you listening to me?''

''Yup.''

''That's perfect,'' she crowed. ''You stick to saying that with an occasional 'Howdy, ma'am' and we'll make a fortune. Aren't you excited?''

Greg rose to his feet. ''The only part that excites me is your research. I can hardly wait for the results of that.''

''Research?'' Stacy asked blankly. Intent on needling Greg, she hadn't paid any attention to her own babbling.

''On famous ladies of the evening.'' Standing behind her, he dropped his hands to her shoulders. ''Maybe you might learn something,'' he unleashed a wicked grin in the mirror, ''useful.''

Stacy's heart skipped a beat. She was still clad only in the towel and Greg's long callused fingers were brown against her pale skin. And warm. Her gaze traveled up. The gray eyes that met hers were filled with mockery. Gregory Ferris was no more worried about what Stacy intended than a full-grown bull worried about a kitten playing in his pasture. Stacy immediately took offense. "You're not taking me seriously."

"You know I'll never turn the ranch into some fancy dude outfit. You're only trying to rile me." He smoothed his palms over her bare shoulders. "But you're going about it wrong."

"I certainly am." She glared at him in the mirror. The nerve of him, trying to seduce her into forgetting that he was a lying, cheating skunk. "It's nothing to me how you raise the money to buy me out. I'll give you three months to come up with the cash. If you haven't paid me by then, I'll put my share of the ranch on the open market."

"C.B. never intended for any of the ranch to go to outsiders." Greg's fingers bit into her shoulders.

"I know what C.B. intended, but he's dead, so this is between you and me. Three months." That wiped the amusement from his face. The bedroom door slammed shut with a vengeance. It appeared that Greg was finally ready to take her seriously. The satisfaction gained by besting him was somehow missing. Stacy absently rubbed the red marks on her shoulders. Greg was interested in seducing her for one reason and one reason only. He wanted her share of the ranch.

Greg's pounding on the door the next morning awakened Stacy. She didn't have to open her eyes to know dawn had yet to appear on the horizon. Greg would never miss an opportunity to roust her out of bed in the middle of the night. She threw back the covers and sat up, shivering in the dark room. What little sleep she'd managed had been hard won, her mind persisting in toying with the question of what might have happened if she hadn't thrown her ultimatum in Greg's face. Stupid. One couldn't turn back the clock. Standing up, she groaned. Her body was stiff from yesterday's unaccustomed long ride. What cruel and inhuman punishment did Greg have in mind for her this morning? Shoveling out stalls, no doubt.

Stacy tightened the belt that held up C.B.'s old jeans. Greg had trapped her nicely, accusing her of being a baby incapable of handling her own problems. Stupidly she'd fallen for the challenge. As he'd known she would. One wondered what he hoped to accomplish by insisting that, as part-owner, she had to share the work. He surely couldn't think putting her to work would have any effect on her desire to sell the ranch.

He'd disabled her car, so he couldn't be trying to drive her away. Yet there was nothing to be gained by keeping her here. Except as an outlet for his frustration. C.B. had wronged Greg by willing part of the ranch to Stacy. And now Greg's scheme to obtain Stacy's share by staying married to her had blown up in his face. Stacy smoothed her hair over her forehead. Greg's actions last night proved he hadn't learned his lesson.

Greg and breakfast were waiting in the kitchen. One look at Greg's closed face made it clear that pleasant conversation over coffee was out. Stacy ate in silence, begrudgingly admitting that, no matter how early Greg had awakened her, he must have risen even earlier to dress and prepare breakfast. Now he was wrapping food to take with him.

Not him. Them. Rio was a large, dark shape at the corral but Stacy could sense his alert awareness of them. He trotted briskly over at her whistle. The stallion was saddled. Greg had been busy. Wordlessly Stacy accepted the apple Greg handed her. There was just enough light for Stacy to recognize the white blazed face of Greg's brown gelding, Arkansas, before Greg swung up into the saddle and led the way from the corral.

Farther down the Valley a ghostly fog hovered at the base of the Sangre de Cristos. Snorting clouds of steam, the two horses picked their way in the dark. Their hoofs thudded against the white-frosted ground or struck an occasional rock. Metal clinked and leather creaked. Familiar sounds to Stacy. Companionable sounds. Or they would be if it weren't for the dark, silent figure ahead of her.

Greg reined Arkansas to a halt and pointed wordlessly toward the creek. Two mule deer stood in the half light of dawn, their ears pricked toward the horses and riders. The faint lowing of cattle carried on the early morning breeze. "C.B.'s dad, my great-grandfather, started this spread." Greg rested his forearm on the saddle horn and looked around. "He didn't have much money but he worked long and hard to make this land into something he considered useful. C.B. was only fourteen the year his dad was killed by a rogue horse. Fourteen, the eldest of eight kids and man of the family. He told me once he couldn't get married until all the kids were settled. Didn't want to wish the raising of his sisters and brothers on a wife. Then his mother, I guess she was a strong-minded woman, not the kind to sit back and let a younger woman run what had been her house. By the time she died, C.B. said he was too set in his ways to marry."

"I'm glad he had you," Stacy said honestly.

Greg flicked the ends of the reins against his jeans-clad leg. "He told me once he never regretted doing what he felt was right but admitted he'd had a 'powerful hankering' for a wife and family of his own. His brothers and sisters left the ranch as soon as they were old enough to head for the city and one by one C.B. bought them out. Of course, he told them they were to consider the ranch their home as long as they wanted."

Stacy remembered the hordes of nieces and nephews who periodically descended on C.B. C.B. had housed them, fed them, entertained them and mounted them on his gentlest horses. All had been invited to stay for a summer or winter of ranch living. All had politely declined and returned to the cities and towns from whence they'd come. "Nobody ever loved this place like you and C.B.," she said.

"Which is why the ranch belongs to me," Greg said. "Not in the sense that one owns a book or a chair. I've been given the privilege of living here and the responsibility of taking care of the land to the best of my ability." He waved his arm in a sweeping arc. "Taking care of it means rotating cows so they don't destroy the pastures beyond recovery. Making the waterholes available to the deer and pronghorns as well as the cattle and horses. Leaving some underbrush for pheasants and ptarmigan and rabbits. Even coyotes are part of Mother Nature's plan." He nudged Arkansas into a shambling walk.

Stacy followed, her brow creased in thought. Greg seldom did anything without a purpose. C.B. had told her more than once that she was too impatient. When Greg wanted her to know a thing, he'd tell her.

The sky was pearly gray and below them windows glowed with light as the Valley woke from sleep. Dawn outlined the Sangre de Cristos in red. Ahead of her, Greg reined in. "The sandhill cranes are mostly gone now. South into New Mexico. After all these years I still get a thrill in September when I hear their peculiar call and look up to see the first ones flying overhead en route to Monte Vista. I drove by the refuge the other day and saw four whooping cranes in one spot. One day last March I saw two whoopers in a grain field and half a dozen bald eagles in trees along side the same field. Two of the world's endangered species and I saw them both the same day." He shrugged. "Not uncommon here in the Valley in the spring."

Stacy couldn't contain herself any longer. "You didn't drag me out here for a lecture on Mother Nature."

Greg shoved his hat to the back of his head and slouched lazily in his saddle, his hands resting on the horn. "Your dad's been thinking about what happens to his ranch when he's gone."

"That's a long way in the future."

"Let's hope so. Meanwhile, I've about worked out a deal with him to lease the place and run his cattle. He's putting it all in a trust for your kids."

The sun popped over the peaks. The ice-rimmed leaves of a yucca plant glittered diamond bright in the cold sunlight. "I don't suppose that has anything to do with you refusing to give me a divorce," Stacy said slowly.

Greg's eyes narrowed dangerously. "If you were a man, Slim, I'd slug you for a remark like that."

"If I've come to any conclusions you don't like, you have only yourself to thank. And you didn't answer my question of why we're out here."

"You walked away from your dad's place without a backward glance." He surveyed the Valley. "I thought you might need reminding of what you're so eager to get rid of, city lady."

"I see." Anger rose in waves, blurring the landscape around her. Greg had lied to her and tried to cheat her. Then he'd puffed up like an angry horned toad when she'd questioned his intent, and now he had the nerve to... She clamped down hard on her trembling lower lip. C.B. had been wrong to will part of the ranch away from Greg. Anyone with a sense of right and wrong could see that. So what did that make her in Greg's eyes?

She turned Rio toward the ranch house. If she was crying, her tears were tears of rage. Greg hadn't trusted her to do the right thing. Her stomach twisted with the pain of betrayal. He should have known her better. He should have known she would turn the ranch over to him. You tried to convince him otherwise, an inner voice reminded her. Stacy urged Rio into a trot. Greg had started it with his lying and cheating. If he'd come to her at the beginning with the truth, but no... Instead he'd gone on the offensive as if she were some avaricious, grasping stranger out to steal his birthright from him.

At the corral she jumped down from Rio's back and turned to Greg. "You've got three months," she said in a voice shaking with anger. "Three months to come up with the money or I'll find a developer who'll turn your deer and antelope playground into one-acre lots."

Greg looped Arkansas's reins over the top railing of the corral and walked toward her. "You don't mean that."

"Don't I? Then you have nothing to worry about, do you?" She swung around on her heel.

A long arm yanked her back to face him. "Dammit, Slim," his eyes smoldered down at her, "the reasonable thing to do is stay married and——"

"Reasonable!" she spat furiously. "How dare you ca
staying married to a lying hypocrite like you reason
able?"

"I dare," he bit out, "because you're my wife." H
crushed her up against his body.

The kiss was hard and possessive and filled with
strange urgency. Stacy knew her face was as white a
Greg's when he finally released her. Every muscle in he
body trembling with betrayal and outrage, she stare
stonily up at him. "Three months or next year you
precious whooping cranes can eat at backyard bird
feeders for all I care." Over her shoulder, she added
"I'm taking one of your cars and I swear, if you try an
stop me, I'll run you down. With pleasure." Minute
later she tore from the yard, leaving Greg staring afte
her, a rare look of ill-tempered frustration on his face

Even so late in the day, it felt more like September i
Colorado Springs than November, with pedestrian
warmed by the last rays of the setting sun before th
fiery orb dropped behind Pikes Peak. Limp, brow
autumn leaves, damp from melted snow, lined the stree
and perfumed the air. Deep in discussion with Stan, Stac
turned into the parking lot. A second later she came t
a confused halt.

"What's the matter?" Stan asked.

"I don't see my car." A maroon sedan now occupie
the space where she'd parked Greg's car that morning
She scanned the area with puzzled eyes. A car doo
opened and slammed shut.

"Isn't that it? Over there with your husband?"

Stacy turned startled eyes in the direction Stan wa
looking. Greg was leaning against the hood of her ca
Her car keys dangled from his finger. Bidding Sta

goodbye in an automatic voice, Stacy walked forward slowly. She stopped a few paces from Greg. "Where's your car?"

"I drove your car up this afternoon and traded it for mine. I'd just started back to the ranch when a passing truck spit gravel and cracked my windshield. My car's over at the glass place now."

"And I suppose you need a ride over there." She lifted the keys from him.

"Actually, I need a little more than that." He held her door, preventing her from closing it. "My car won't be ready until morning. I thought I'd bunk down at your place."

"You're wasting your time. I'm going to sell and nothing you say will change my mind."

Greg walked around and slid into the passenger side of the car. "Don't tell me that fellow's wife is out of town again."

"Of course," Stacy snapped. "We can hardly sleep together when she's in town."

"I wouldn't have said he was your type." Greg stretched his legs out in front of him.

"It's a little late for you to play the jealous husband."

"Jealous? Of that guy? In that pinstriped suit and vest, all he needs is a bowler hat and umbrella to look like——"

"The perfect banker."

"I was thinking more along the lines of Charlie Chaplin."

"Very amusing." There was no doubt in Stacy's mind that Greg's disparaging remark was intended more to demonstrate his uninterest in her social life than to belittle Stan.

Greg rested his arm along the back of the seat. "Knowing how inexperienced you are, I'd be happy to give you some advice on picking my successor."

"I can manage my life perfectly well without you." Forgetting she'd started the car, she turned the key again. The car whined in protest.

"I can tell," Greg said in a deadpan voice.

Fuming, Stacy nosed the car into the heavy downtown traffic. After a few minutes she said, "You mentioned your successor. Does that mean you've finally come to your senses and are willing to let me get a divorce? Now that I know about C.B.'s will, there's no reason for you to fight the divorce."

"One has nothing to do with the other."

"Come off it, Greg," Stacy fought her way onto the interstate. "You know very well the only reason you opposed the divorce is because you knew it'd come out that C.B. left me part of the ranch."

"I told you you could have your divorce."

"With one condition."

"With one condition," Greg agreed.

"That's blackmail."

"What do you call a threat to sell your share of the ranch in three months?"

"Justice," Stacy retorted.

Greg laughed and pulled his hat low to shield his eyes from the blazing sunset. "Since when is justice another word for getting even?"

"All right. Call it revenge if you want. At least I'm honest enough to admit I'm angry."

"Meaning I'm not honest enough. What makes you think I'm angry?"

"Your stupid condition." Stacy pulled into her townhouse garage. "Why else would you insist I sleep with you?"

Greg pushed back his hat and slowly inspected the length of her body. "When you came around the corner this afternoon, there wasn't a man in the vicinity who didn't turn to watch you stride past. No prissy little city steps for you. Those long legs of yours were covering ground."

Stacy shut her car door. "So?"

Greg unfurled his long legs from the front seat of the car and rose to his full height. "Maybe I'm thinking about how those long legs would look in my bed."

Stacy looked sharply at him. The dark shadows in the garage concealed his face. "I don't believe you," she said flatly.

Reaching up, Greg pulled her garage door shut. "I didn't think you would," he said. Taking her keys from her, he unlocked her front door.

Hours later Stacy stood at her bedroom window looking out into the darkened night. Before her the lights of Colorado Springs stretched east to the plains. Cars on the interstate flowed steadily north and south, their headlights and taillights forming parallel red and white streamers. Off in the distance tiny, blinking dots of light turned south, airplanes headed for the airport. Planes filled with passengers, each with a destination in mind. She wished she knew where she was going.

From the spare bedroom came an abrupt sound and Greg swore quietly. A half smile touched her lips. An awkwardly placed electric outlet meant guests were always crashing into the furniture in the dark. Creaking springs told her that Greg had finally gone to bed.

Finally. The evening had been interminable. After arguing over dinner, they'd sent out for pizza. His, regular crust with everything; hers, vegetarian with wholewheat crust. She'd practically drooled every time he'd lifted a piece of his, but no way she'd admit she only ordered hers because he'd called it "yuppie" pizza and said that he supposed it was what a city girl like her would eat. Her friends would have laughed to see her drinking wine with her pizza. But not for a million dollars would she have drunk a beer as Greg did. The smile on her face broadened. Suffering through the pizza was a small price to pay for the privilege of seeing the look on Greg's face when she pulled out the video of a foreign movie and said she'd been dying to see it. Someone had given her the video last Christmas as a joke and it was totally incomprehensible, with subtitles that bore little relation to what was happening on the screen.

Of course, she'd been too aware of Greg to concentrate on a stupid movie. Greg shifted his body. Her walls were inordinately thin. The only reason she'd insisted on watching the movie was to annoy Greg. Well, maybe that wasn't the only reason. Or even the real reason. The movie was safe. As long as they were occupied watching it, they couldn't talk. She couldn't blurt out the one hundred and one questions that she wanted Greg to answer. Like why he was insisting she sleep with him before he'd let her get the divorce. She knew darned good and well it had nothing to do with her legs or he would have tried to convince her when she'd said she didn't believe him. Instead, he was positively uninterested in what she did or didn't believe. Positively uninterested in her.

Her past was entwined with Greg. It was time she created a future without him. Her friend Molly at the bank had gone back east for a master's degree in business and still raved about the experience. Maybe that's what she ought to do. Become a career woman. Go to Harvard University in Massachusetts. Trade chinook winds for sea breezes. Replace the sound of western drawls with Bostonian accents. No cows and no horses. No Greg.

With her finger she sketched a face in the condensation on the inside of the window. The corners of the mouth turned down. Greg was always accusing her of still being a child. The adult thing to do was to stop this foolishness about the ranch and tell him that she had no intention of doing anything with her share of the ranch except turn it over to him. Maybe then they could clear up this nonsense about their marriage and divorce once and for all. Greg was wrong to try and trick her into staying married to him, but in a way, she understood. The ranch was his life and she threatened that life. It was no wonder he'd gone a little crazy. Once she explained to him what her intentions were, they could laugh about the misunderstanding. Maybe, she thought wistfully, they could even part friends.

From next door came the sound of creaking bedsprings again. He was still awake. She'd tell him now. There was no sense in putting it off. If she was going to start a new life, she might as well start.

The door to her guest bedroom stood partially open. Drawn curtains failed to totally block the light from a nearby street lamp. Stacy quietly eased the door open wider. Greg was sprawled facedown across the bed. A stray beam of light showed his back moving rhythmically in and out with the steady cadence of a sound sleeper. Stacy fumbled behind her for the door.

"What's the matter?"

"I didn't mean to wake you." She stood awkwardly inside the door, suddenly wishing she'd left this discussion until morning. Greg's upper torso was bare.

"I wasn't asleep." Greg sat up in bed, settling the blankets across his middle. "What's on your mind?"

"Nothing." She took a step backward. "I didn't mean to bother you."

"You didn't. Come here." He patted the bed beside him. "Let's talk."

She shook her head. "No. It's late."

"Don't make me come after you." Greg's voice stopped her backward retreat. "Although if you can do it, so can I."

The amusement in his voice puzzled her. "Do what?"

"Streak," he said.

"Streak? Oh." Greg was warning her he was nude beneath the covers. She stood indecisively in the doorway, mentally taking stock of the stupid situation she'd got herself into. Greg was perfectly capable of nakedly chasing her through the house. It seemed safer to humor him. Stacy walked across the carpeted room and perched gingerly on the edge of the mattress. "I'm really not in the mood for talking." She forced a yawn. "I'm awfully sleepy. I'd better go back to bed."

"No, you don't." Greg yanked on her shoulder, toppling her on her back. He leaned over her as she stared up at him in surprise. "Now talk. Why are you wandering the halls in the middle of the night?"

"I couldn't sleep and I thought I'd check to see if you were warm enough," she said, rapidly improvising.

"What's keeping you awake?" Propping a pillow against the headboard, he leaned back. "Problems?"

"Yes." Sitting up, Stacy gave him a look of pure disgust, "I have a husband I can't get rid of." Folding up her legs, she hugged her knees to her chest. The less room she took up, the less chance she'd brush against Greg.

Greg laughed. "You're just cranky because your muscles are sore. I noticed how gingerly you sat down at the table. You're not used to riding as much as you did this past weekend." Moving behind her, he brushed his knuckles against the nape of her neck. "You've turned into a soft city girl."

"I have not."

"Relax," he ordered, rubbing his palm up and down her spine. "No wonder you couldn't sleep. You're stiff as a board." He massaged her upper back and shoulders, his thumbs digging deep into her knotted muscles.

His hands were warm and callused. Stacy could feel the strength flowing through them. She squeaked in protest as Greg vigorously kneaded the muscles around her neck. His fingers weren't so much soothing her muscles as adamantly insisting the muscles relax. "Hey, don't take your frustrations out on me," she said, half teasing, "just because C.B. left me part of your ranch." She ought to tell him now about the ranch. The tension eased from her muscles as Greg worked his fingers up and down her backbone. She'd tell him in just a minute.

Greg shoved her legs to one side and pushed her down on her stomach. "Since you're so all-fired anxious to be free of this marriage, maybe we can come to an agreement. What do you say?"

Stacy turned her head to look up at him. Difficult to do when lying on one's stomach with one's muscles being brutally pummeled by a battering ram. "What did you have in mind?" she asked cautiously.

"Your share of the ranch for a divorce." Greg's eyes glittered in the light from the street lamp.

This was her cue to tell him that she intended to give him her share in the ranch, but the desire to do the right thing evaporated in the face of Greg's insistence on seeing her in the worst possible light. ''That's dirty pool,'' she said in a low, fierce voice. ''Not that I expect anything better of you.'' His low opinion of her hurt bitterly. For him to believe that she would actually steal his inheritance and then use what she'd stolen as a bargaining chip to regain her freedom . . . it was the ultimate insult. She exploded with anger. ''You've been acting like a horse's behind ever since I said I wanted a divorce. You've threatened me, made ultimatums. You didn't tell me C.B. left me part of the ranch. You kidnapped me, wrecked my car and tried to cheat me but I never thought you'd sink this low. You can't claim I did one thing to influence C.B. to give me part of the ranch. I could have told him we were married. He would have given me half the ranch if he'd known. But I didn't. I played fair.'' She glared furiously at him. ''Name one thing I've done to you.''

''Married me.''

CHAPTER NINE

STACY froze, unable to deny Greg's quiet words. It all came down to this. Everything that had happened was her fault. She'd insisted he sleep with her and when she'd gone to him, fearing she was pregnant, Greg had heard her out in silence, no word of blame passing his lips. If he'd lost his temper after their abortive marriage, berating her for the mess in which she'd landed them, she could hardly blame him. Because of her Greg had borne the burden of a secret marriage at the same time as he was carrying the twin loads of C.B.'s illness and the responsibility of the ranch. And then, the ultimate blow, Stacy inheriting part of the ranch. No wonder Greg was behaving totally out of character. The past three years were enough to warp any man's personality. "I know it's all my fault," she said in a little voice. "I—I thought I was crazy in love with you, but that's not much of an excuse. It was a pretty selfish love. I wanted you and I didn't care what you wanted." Staring blindly at the pillow, she added quietly, "I know it's a little late, but for what it's worth I'm sorry for all the pain and distress and trouble I caused you."

Greg's hands were still. "It's not too late." He slid his hands under her pajama top. "Not that I'm letting you claim all the blame."

Stacy could feel the calloused pads on his thumbs as he massaged the small of her back. "I started the whole mess." The painful knots were gone from her muscles but a new tension was stealing over her.

Greg slid down the mattress, stretching his long body out beside hers, securing the sheet between them. "We both started it." No longer massaging, he trailed his hand over her back. "Maybe we should kiss and make up." He drew circles on her skin.

Her stomach dipped. "Maybe we should," she recklessly mumbled into the pillow. Her thin pajamas were no barrier to the heat put out by Greg's body.

"You first." Greg settled on his back, the sheet wrapped around his waist.

Turning toward him, Stacy propped herself up on her elbow. "Why me?"

He sent a slow smile her way. "You said yourself you started it." He ran a forefinger over her bottom lip. "It seems fair for you to start the kiss of apology."

Stacy eyed him uncertainly. Her lips felt warm and bee-stung. "I guess I owe you that much." He made no other move toward her, seemingly content to lie by her side. "Just one kiss?"

He folded his arms across his chest. "If you can't stop at one——" closing his eyes, he screwed up his face, his lips pursed in a parody of a kiss "—I'm a man. I can take all the kisses you want to throw at me."

Stacy punched his chin lightly. "I'm more likely to throw a boot at you."

"A city sophisticate like you?" He opened one eye. "I never thought I'd meet a banker who didn't pay her debts."

"That sounds like a challenge to me."

"Does it?" Greg studied her thoughtfully out of his one opened eye. "The Slim I used to know accepted at the drop of a hat every challenge that came her way." He paused. "But I suppose when you moved to the big city you lost your nerve."

Stacy met his one-eyed stare. "The day I lose my nerve is the day you lose your arrogance. And we all know the sky'll fall before that happens."

"In that case..." Greg closed his eye, an expectant look on his face.

Stacy leaned down and brushed her lips across the surface of his warm mouth. "There."

Greg squinted up at her. "According to you, you owe me for what I've gone through the past three years. Seems to me a considerable amount of interest must have built up."

"Who's the banker here, you or me?"

"I'm just a man collecting a debt."

"Charging usurious interest," she retorted.

His slow smile mocked her. "I suppose you think big words disguise the fact that you've turned into a sissy city lady."

"I have not," Stacy said. Greg's raised eyebrow clearly expressed polite disbelief. Mentally squaring her shoulders, she took hold of Greg's wrists and pushed his arms over his head and held them there. On her knees, she looked down at him. "You want to take that back or do I have to prove I'm no sissy?"

Greg's grey eyes were dark and intent. "Prove it."

Stacy lowered her head. Greg's lips were dry and roughened by hours of outside labour. She moistened them with the tip of her tongue. Greg lay perfectly still. Stacy curled her tongue and drew a wet line around his mouth. Drawn to the corners of his mouth, she pressed tiny kisses there. His skin was warm, and his cheeks smelled of after-shave tinged with the freshness of out-doors. Turning her head slightly, she fluttered her long eyelashes across the fullness of his cheek, at the same time releasing his wrists and sliding her hands along the length of his sinewy arms. The well-toned muscles flexed beneath her fingers.

"Call me a sissy city lady, will you?" she said softly into his ear. Greg might be rawhide and steel and barbed wire but his earlobe was soft and pliable between her lips. Unlike his jaw, which might have been shaped from stone. Except his jaw was warm, not cold. Stacy scattered kisses along his jawline from one ear to another. She laughed softly back in her throat as she ran her hands over his bare shoulders, enjoying the feel of well-toned muscles. Greg was motionless, the only signs of life about him his harsh breathing and the pulse at the base of his neck which seemed to beat faster as she pressed her mouth against it.

Moistening her lips, Stacy braced her forearms on Greg's chest and slowly covered his mouth with hers. She parted her lips slightly and feathered her tongue over his closed mouth. Greg's breathing quickened. Slowly she drew the tip of her tongue between his lips from one corner of his mouth to the other and back again. There was a slight chill to the bedroom air but Greg's body was a furnace heating her flesh through her pajamas. With a soft sigh Stacy slid her tongue between his welcoming lips. He tasted of the beer he'd had with dinner.

Greg scraped his teeth lightly around the perimeter of her tongue and then his tongue met hers and any illusion that she was in command fled. He wove his fingers through her hair and pressed fiercely against her scalp, holding her mouth locked against his. His kiss was wet and deep and thorough.

When he finally released her Stacy was shaking from the intensity of the kiss. She could scarcely hold up her head and tried twice to find her voice before she finally managed to ask with false assurance, "Are you ready to concede that I'm as tough as I ever was?"

"I'll concede——" with a quick roll of his body he flipped her on her back beneath him "—that you're one hell of a city lady." His head blotted out the light from the street lamp. The sheet was no longer tucked between them.

Morning light streamed around the edges of the drawn curtains. Greg's after-shave clung to the bedsheets. Stacy lay motionless on her back, staring at the ceiling. She didn't need to turn her head to know she was alone in the bed, but even if the pillow beside her was empty it would bear the imprint of Greg's head. As her body seemed to bear the imprint of his body.

She had spent the night in Greg's bed. In Greg's arms. They had fitted together as comfortably as a pair of well-worn shoes, exploring each other's bodies with grace and a freedom from embarrassment. Stacy's spare bedroom was no sleazy motel room and she was no longer a virgin teenager. She and Greg were adults. Last night moving from apology to kiss to making love had seemed right and natural.

With the morning had come the humiliating realization that her enthusiastic response in his bed last night must have astonished Greg. She had come to his room to give him back his ranch. She had stayed to give him something quite different. There was no shying away from the truth. Whatever Greg had expected when she'd kissed him last night, she doubted very much if his expectations had included Stacy exploding into a creature of passion and demanding desires. Memories of the night replayed themselves in her mind with embarrassing clarity, the molten images curling her toes with shame.

And rekindling the desire. Beneath the covers she dug her fingers deep into the mattress.

Greg had worshiped her body with his hands and mouth, and the softly drawled words of appreciation for legs and breasts had flowed over her body like warm golden honey. Yet, for all the enjoyment they'd given and received, Stacy could not blind herself to the fact that there had been one significant omission. They'd shared passion, but Greg had made no mention of a shared future. He'd had spoken no words of love and, if Stacy knew one thing, it was that if those words were to be spoken this time they had to be spoken first by Greg.

"I know you keep bankers' hours, but all the same you'd better get up."

Stacy turned her head. Greg stood in the doorway wearing the same jeans and sweatshirt he'd worn yesterday. His feet were bare. He drank from an old mug she'd found in an antiques store, holding the mug so that the gaudy buckaroo decoration was visible across the room. The aroma of coffee eddied into the room. Stubble, not unattractive, darkened his cheeks and chin. The details seared themselves on her brain even as she forced herself to meet Greg's gaze. His gray eyes were wary. "The coffee smells good," she said.

"I'll bring you a cup."

"No!" The panic in her voice was all too plain. She tried again. "I'll come down to the kitchen." She remembered her state of undress. "In a few minutes."

"All right." Greg disappeared from the doorway.

Disappointment sat painfully on her chest. Fool, she mentally scoffed. What did she expect? Greg was probably terrified she'd read something into what had happened. He wanted one thing from her—his ranch.

What he didn't want was Stacy. She blinked away hot tears of humiliation. He'd made both desires very clear last night when he'd offered her a divorce in exchange for her ranch shares. Their making love last night was obviously nothing more to him than a way of sealing their bargain. She hadn't been making love; she'd been signing on the dotted line.

Stacy dragged her body from the bed. Her immediate hurdle was dealing with Greg, persuading him that the evening meant nothing more to her than it did to him. Later, when he'd gone, she'd deal calmly and rationally with the truth.

"Sleep okay?" he asked as she walked into the kitchen.

Showered and dressed, she felt armored against whatever the morning threw at her. "Of course." Dawn was graying the sky before she'd fallen into deep, satisfied slumber. "And you?"

"Best sleep I've had in a long time."

The thread of amusement in his voice flustered her and she reached for the morning paper.

"The forecast is chilly with a hint of snow."

"It says here we're to have a sunny day." She riffled the edges of the paper with her thumb, not meeting his gaze.

"I wasn't referring to the weather."

His dry voice brought her head up. "I—I thought you were," she said inanely, gulping at the coffee he handed her. He'd added exactly the right amount of cream and for a moment she was transported back to C.B.'s kitchen, she and Greg and C.B. drinking huge mugs of coffee to take the chill off after a cold, wet ride. "My mother would have a fit if she knew C.B. gave coffee to a ten-year-old."

"Are we going to talk about it?"

"C.B. giving me coffee?" She knew very well Greg wasn't referring to coffee.

Greg set a plate of eggs on the counter in front of where she sat perched on a stool. "You didn't used to be a coward," he said deliberately.

Stacy slowly picked up her fork. "All right. I enjoyed last night." She pressed her thumb against the pointed tines of the fork.

"That's it?" Greg asked evenly.

"No, that's not it." She slid the cool metal fork between her fingers. "I was angry about your condition for the divorce, but now I... You were right to insist that we needed to sleep with each other in order to satisfactorily close the book on our relationship." Aimlessly she stirred the coffee with the handle of her fork. "The first time, well, it was unsatisfactory, and I suppose I did blame you for that, but all the same... I feel better knowing that I'm not a complete failure in bed." She risked a quick peek at him. His face gave no clue to his thoughts.

"That sounds a lot like goodbye."

"I've decided to move back east. Go back to school."

"When did you decide that?" Greg asked tightly.

"Last night."

"Before or after you hopped into my bed?"

The anger in his voice warned her against disputing his version. Even if he was the one who'd insisted she sit on the bed, she wasn't totally blameless. He hadn't forced her to leave her room and go to his. He was still waiting for an answer. "Before."

"I think we've played this scene before," Greg said in a hard voice. "You seduce me and then run away."

She stared at her coffee, fighting for control as the painful memories assailed her. "You sent me away," she

finally said in a monotone. "You told me to go away."
She looked at him then. "That I'd pestered you beyond
what a man could endure."

Greg studied her intently across the table. "I don't
remember," he said slowly. "I just remember you
crying."

Stacy shrugged away his loss of memory but that didn't
stop the hurt. His angry words had slashed deeply into
her heart and he didn't even remember. Which only
proved how unimportant the words were to him. How
unimportant she was to him. She stared down at her
plate. "I believe we had a deal." The yellow eggs sat in
a watery pool. Her toast was burned. She'd been meaning
to have the toaster fixed. "You agreed to a divorce if I
slept with you once." The room hummed with tension.
Stacy bit into her toast with a loud crunch. "I'll see a
lawyer as soon as possible." The toast was a mistake.
Her throat muscles refused to work. She needed a large
swallow of coffee to wash down the dry, tasteless
mouthful. "I hope I can count on you to keep your word
now that I've given you what you want."

"What makes you so sure I've got what I want?"

Stacy made a halfhearted gesture with her fork.
"About the ranch——"

"Shut up," Greg ground out between his teeth. "Just
shut up." Standing in front of her, he grabbed her
shoulders and hauled her to her feet, his fingers pressing
deep into her flesh.

Her fork clattered to the floor. "If you're going——"

"I'm going," he said grimly. "But not before I kiss
the almost ex-Mrs. Ferris goodbye."

Long before her brain could muster any reason why
he shouldn't kiss her, he'd covered her lips with his. By

the time Stacy remembered how dangerous Greg's kisses were, his hands had slid down her back to cup her hips tightly against his and his tongue was arrogantly claiming her mouth. Even worse, her fingers were thrust into his hair, holding his lips locked to hers. Common sense told her responding was a disastrous mistake, but she refused to listen. Even a condemned man gets a last request, she thought defiantly, and then all rational thought fled before lips and fingers that had learned all her secrets the previous night. By the time Greg strolled out of the door, her pride was in shreds, her clothing in total disarray, her muscles turned to limp gelatine. "Damn it, even my eggs are cold," Stacy said loudly, the words echoing in the empty apartment. And then she burst into tears.

Tears were a weakness she had no intention of repeating, she told herself as she slammed her car door two days later in front of the one-story stucco building which housed Les Craddock's law office. A huge semi-truck pulling a trailer loaded high with large bales of alfalfa rumbled past raising a cloud of dust. Half a dozen sparrows exploded from a bush beside the walk as Stacy headed toward the office door. Greg would be waiting inside. If she had any doubts about Greg wanting this divorce, the speed with which he'd arranged their appointment with Les would have quickly disabused her of such a foolish notion. They were meeting today to set into motion the wheels of their divorce. The sooner the better, Greg had blandly announced over the telephone. The other night he had protected them against the very scare that three years ago had stampeded them into their disastrous marriage. Stacy blinked back hot tears. He'd made very sure that there was absolutely no obstacle to their obtaining a divorce.

"No obstacle at all," she repeated firmly to Les Craddock minutes later. "The marriage is irretrievably and irrevocably severed due to irreconcilable differences or whatever the legal mumbo jumbo is."

Les looked over his glasses at Greg. "You agree?"

"It was a mistake from the start," Greg said positively.

Stacy swallowed hard. "Before we go any further," she clutched the bag lying in her lap, "I want to go on record as refusing to accept any settlement from Greg. I also want to sign over to him the share in the ranch that C.B. left me in his will." She sensed Greg's sudden immobility at her side.

The lawyer was shaking his head. "Greg is prepared to be very generous," he began.

"Greg is always generous." Les's law degree hung on the wall next to a Remington print. "The fact remains that C.B. always intended that the ranch belong to Greg."

"Don't be hasty," Les said. "I think you ought to get yourself a lawyer, Stacy." He glanced over at Greg. "I know you wanted us to handle this without outsiders, Greg, and you and C.B. have been my clients for years, but I don't like——"

"You can act for Slim, Les. I don't need a lawyer."

"That's not what I was going to say. If Stacy signs away all her rights now, she can't go back to the courts later and say she's changed your mind. Waiving maintenance is a permanent waiver. I'd like her to think about it."

"I won't change my mind." From the corner of her eye, Stacy could see Greg's long legs stretched out in front of him as he leaned back in the chair beside her. "Another lawyer wouldn't make a bit of difference. I refuse to take one penny from Greg."

"No judge——"

Stacy interrupted the lawyer. "Neither he nor anyone else can make me take anything from Greg. I don't want anything. I never wanted his money. I never spent the allowance he sent me." She turned to Greg. "I want you to quit sending me money and to take back everything you sent. I don't need your money. I can take care of myself."

"I'll quit sending it." Greg brushed a bit of dust from the brim of his hat. "But you'll keep what I've already sent you."

"No."

He turned his hat and brushed the other side. "Then no divorce."

"I don't want your money."

"I said you'll keep it." His eyes blazed at her, more black then gray.

Stacy backed down. She could argue that point later. "I'm not keeping the share in the ranch that C.B. left me."

"I urge you to reconsider," Les said in a troubled voice. "Any division of property is final."

"Leave her alone," Greg said. "Once Slim's made up her mind to something, a truckload of dynamite isn't going to sway her."

"Naturally it's in your best interest, Greg, for Stacy to feel this way," Les said, "but I'm not sure——"

"I'm sure." Stacy said automatically. She'd come prepared to argue with Greg over her intentions and his prompt acceptance of her relinquishing any claim to the ranch or his income stung. If he'd drawn a picture, he couldn't have made it clearer exactly why he'd been fighting the divorce. He must feel like jumping with glee. Not only was he shedding an unwanted wife, it wasn't costing him a penny and he was getting his ranch back.

The last, tiny remnant of her stupid, secret dream withered away. She cleared her throat. "All I want you to do, Les, is to write up the papers the way I said and do all the necessary filing. If you refuse, I'll find someone else."

Les Craddock made a frustrated gesture before clasping his hands on the surface of his huge wooden desk. "I don't like it."

"You don't have to like it," Greg said.

A piercing pain stabbed the back of Stacy's eyeballs, but the anguish of broken dreams wasn't going to defeat her now. "How long before we're divorced?" She beat Greg to the question. The anticipation in his voice would be unbearable.

"Now, Stacy," the lawyer's face was concerned, "I'd like——"

"How long?"

Les sighed. "I'll take care of the paperwork and you'll have to come back and sign it. I'll file the petition for dissolution with the courts and set a date for your final hearing. You have to wait ninety days before your hearing. At that time, you can get your name legally changed back to your maiden name, Stacy, if you want."

"I do." She stood up. "Thank you, Les. I appreciate what you tried to do, but I've made up my mind." She turned to Greg who had risen to his feet beside her and blindly stuck out her hand, praying he wouldn't notice the moisture filming over her eyes. "I guess that's it then."

"I want to talk to you." Greg captured her elbow. "Les, do you have a room where we can talk and won't be disturbed for a couple of minutes?"

"You have everything you want," Stacy protested. "There's nothing left to say."

Greg ignored her protest, hauling her along in Les's wake. The room the lawyer ushered them into was obviously the law firm's library. Floor-to-ceiling shelves filled with large, somber books lined the wall. A dark wood table was ringed with wooden chairs. Les switched on the lights and closed the door, shutting them in. At the soft click of the closing door, Greg yanked the nearest chair from under the table and pointed Stacy at it. She sat down stiffly on the chair's edge, her gaze centered on the black ink spots which marred the table's polished surface. Greg stood silently behind her, causing the hair on the back of her neck to prickle uneasily.

"You neglected to mention one piece of property." A ring dropped to the table with a dull thud and lay gleaming in a pool of light from the overhead chandelier.

CHAPTER TEN

THE last time Stacy had seen the ring was when she'd ripped it from her finger at the filling station in Pagosa Springs. A band of pain tightened around her chest. For three years, each time she'd filled her car with gasoline, the pungent fumes had revived bitter memories. "I'd forgotten all about it," she lied.

"No doubt." Greg sat down across the table. "Keep it. It's yours."

"No." She shoved the ring toward him harder than she'd intended. It spun off the table with a glint of gold. "Sorry."

"Are you?" Tapping the table with the fingers of his right hand, he let the ring lie.

Stacy endured the irritating staccato noise as long as she could. "Well?" she demanded. "What did you want to talk about? If you dragged me in here to thank me, forget——"

"I didn't. The ranch was going to be mine, one way or another. This just makes things easier."

"Easier than staying married to me, you mean." Stacy immediately regretted the words. Before Greg could misconstrue her outburst, she added, "Anyway, the joke's on you. If you had told me at the beginning about C.B.'s will, I would have turned my share of the ranch over to you then. I know you deserve the ranch and I don't. I intended to give it back to you all along, only," she glanced at him only to look quickly away when she saw that he was studying her intently, "your lack of trust in me hurt deeply. Three years ago you would have been honest with me.''

"I have never lied to you," Greg said evenly. "There may have been times when I didn't tell you everything and I suppose it's fair to say that I've kept secrets from you, but——" his voice hardened "—never once in all the years we've known each other have I told you a lie."

"You're lying now." Stacy gripped her bag and stood up. Disappointment in Greg cut almost as sharply as the edges of her broken dreams. Her body drooped wearily as she gazed past his wide shoulders. "I just wish when I was ten years old I hadn't known you. I wish I'd never asked you to marry me then or ever. And most of all, I wish when I did, you'd have laughed in my face and said 'hell, no!'" Turning to leave, she added, "The ranch is all yours. There's no reason you have to stay married to me now."

"No reason I have to," he agreed.

She fumbled blindly for the doorknob. "Well——" her laugh was shaky "—see you in court." Greg's hand on her shoulder stopped her. He peeled her hand from the doorknob and dropped something in her palm. She couldn't meet his gaze but her fingers closed involuntarily over the small object.

He raised her closed fist to his mouth and pressed his lips against her curled up fingers. "Trust works both ways." His hand tightened painfully. "You never trusted me, either."

Stacy reached the limits of her control. A desolate sense of loss and despair washed over her and she jerked free of Greg's grip. Dashing down the office hallway, running past the openmouthed receptionist and astonished tenants of the waiting room, she fled for the sanctuary of her car.

"Wait."

Something in Greg's voice compelled her to stop. "What?"

He turned her to face him. "No matter what, Slim," he pressed a warm, lingering kiss against her mouth, "I'll always treasure the friendship we shared."

As Stacy drove out of town, the image of regretful gray eyes was superimposed on the streets and buildings. Greg had kissed their friendship farewell along with their marriage. Friendship. The pallid word hung dismally in the cold interior of her car.

Stacy should have gone home but she couldn't face the pity that would be in her mother's eyes. Suddenly the Valley was an inhospitable place, alien to her. In her town house with its red and black and white city sophistication there'd be no memories of Greg. Except of him lounging in her black leather chair, smiling across the room at her, flirting with her, his eyes smoky as they rested on her legs.

Stacy fought tears all the way over Poncha Pass but south of Buena Vista the highway blurred before her streaming eyes. Passing the turnoff to South Park and Colorado Springs, she crawled into a motel in Buena Vista. Her room was clean and antiseptic and impersonal and there were no neon lights flashing on the walls. She curled up in a ball on the bed, wrapping her fingers so tightly around the gold wedding band in her palm that her fingernails bit deeply into her skin. If only the pain could make her forget that she'd just said goodbye to the man she had loved since she was eight years old. The man she still loved.

Stacy threw the bank statement at her fireplace. A cold front had moved in and it was a good night for a fire.

The statement would make perfect tinder. Starting for the stairs, she thumbed listlessly through her mail. Catalogs and bills. Her foot on the bottom step, she turned with a sigh and, walking over to the fireplace, retrieved the statement from the floor. Burning it was clearly impossible for a person who worked in a bank. Slipping out of her suit jacket, she trudged up the stairs to change her clothes. The tossed statement bounced off the bed and skidded to the floor. She ignored it. Reading it wouldn't change anything. She knew to a penny how much the account contained. Too much. Every month growing. Every month another statement telling her how much interest the money had earned. Every month another reminder of Greg. Every month another reminder that she'd never been more to him than a fiscal responsibility.

Greg and his damned allowance. She should have insisted he take the money back instead of cravenly backing down. The trouble was, she knew darned well that Greg was stubborn enough that he would fight the divorce over some silly principle like that money. She didn't need it. She was perfectly capable of supporting herself. Greg and his antiquated ideas of a husband's role. Heaven knew she'd hardly fulfilled the role of a wife for him. Maybe she could give the money to the future Mrs. Gregory Ferris as a wedding present. The thought almost made her smile. Wouldn't that absolutely infuriate Greg? He couldn't make Stacy take the money back because he would no longer have anything to threaten her with. She could almost hear him forbidding the second Mrs. Ferris to touch the money.

Stacy flung herself on the bed, not caring how badly her skirt wrinkled. On Thursday Les had said ninety days before the final divorce hearing. That left eighty-six days before all ties between her and Greg were severed. No, that wasn't right. She still had to sign the papers next weekend.

Rolling to one side, her eye was caught by the framed photograph. Greg had yet to send the promised picture of Rio by himself. Moving to a sitting position, she picked up the picture and held it tightly to her chest, her eyes closed. The photo was engraved on her mind. The sorrel horse was on a slight knoll, ears alert, head up, sniffing the wind, his tail streaming out behind him. Greg stood by Rio's head, an easy grin on his face, his cowboy hat pushed to the back of his head. Stacy remembered the day she'd taken the picture. It had been Greg's birthday and Rio was wearing the new saddle that C.B. had had especially made as a surprise for Greg.

Greg's birthday. Coming up this Saturday. He'd be thirty-one years old. He couldn't accuse Stacy of not giving him a present. Her signature on the divorce papers would be her gift. No doubt Lucy Fraser would bake him a sugary sweet cake. She probably even knew how to make icing roses. Stacy could bake, but her idea of a cake was something chocolate loaded with nuts. In her opinion menfolk gobbled cake up much too fast to fuss with complicated decorations. An old memory, resurfacing, brought a faint smile to her face. One year she'd baked Greg a birthday cake and decided to decorate it with real flowers. Wildflowers. Only she hadn't washed the flowers and when she'd proudly whipped the cake cover off the cake, it was only to stare in horror at what had seemed like a trillion baby bugs crawling over the cake. Greg had taken one look at the consternation on her face, lopped off the top and trimmed the sides of the cake. Just enough was left for him to have a large piece. Stacy had long suspected that it had taken every bit of Greg's willpower to swallow that cake. But he'd done it and praised her baking talents. Her smile vanished. Lucy Fraser's cake wouldn't have bugs. And it would probably be pink.

Stacy opened the drawer of the bedside table and tossed the photo inside. Facedown. Slamming shut the drawer, she flopped over on her stomach and propped her chin on the back of her hands. The last thing that interested her was the color of cake Lucy baked. Maybe it would be white. Like that damned white envelope still laying on the floor. No wonder her mind was replaying all these stupid memories. Triggered by that maddening statement.

She rolled over and closed her eyes. Unfortunately, shutting her eyes wouldn't make the envelope disappear. If Greg's uncharacteristic behavior over the past couple of weeks had been motivated by revenge, the envelope signified success beyond his wildest dreams. The prospect of a dreary life lay before her, never totally rid of Greg, dogged month after month by this loathsome souvenir of their abortive marriage. Stacy sat bolt upright in bed. She was darned if she was going to let Gregory Ferris continue to control her life. There must be something she could do to rid herself of this albatross of a bank statement. There was no point in running away to the east coast if she couldn't escape this monthly damning reminder of Greg.

Throwing on jeans and a sweatshirt, she went downstairs and fixed herself a cup of herbal tea. After one sip, she dumped the liquid down the drain. Grabbing a beer from her refrigerator, she popped the top and drank straight from the bottle. A pizza, loaded with pepperoni and sausage, went from freezer to oven.

Two hours later, she shoved aside the dirty bowl from her chocolate sundae and laughed out loud. "I've got you, Gregory Ferris, I've got you!" she crowed. The photograph of Rio and Greg sat in the middle of her table, serving as inspiration. Stacy toasted the picture with her mug of coffee. "It's absolutely perfect and I defy you to bully your way out of this. It's downright manipulative, but I learned from a master." Pulling a pad toward her, she jotted down notes for her plan of attack. Gregory Ferris was going to receive the birthday gift of his life.

Anticipating her moment of triumph propelled Stacy through the week. It wasn't until she crested the summit of Poncha Pass on Saturday that the misgivings that had niggled at the back of her mind all week began to surface. The sporty red car was a joy to drive. She almost wished it were hers. Last week in Colorado Springs, giving it to Greg for his birthday had seemed the perfect idea. Secondhand, the car had been a bargain, and she'd bought it with the money Greg had given her over the past three years. The car was registered, licensed and insured in Greg's name. If he didn't want the car, disposal would be up to him, but she was gambling that the physical presence of the car in his yard and the knowledge that it was already his would be Greg's Achilles' heel. Practicality might prevent him from buying a car he coveted, but good manners would compel him to accept a gift. Stacy sniffed experimentally. "But it's a present, Greg," she said out loud. She winced. Maybe a little heavy on the pathos. She tried again. Anything to keep from dwelling on her deepest fear—that Greg might think the car a bribe to get him back.

Greg was standing by the corral saddling Rio. The sorrel gleamed in the sun. "Nice car," Greg said, tightening Rio's girth.

"Thanks." Stacy shut the car door and stood indecisively tossing the car keys from one hand to another. Cravenly she put off what she'd come to do. "What's the occasion?" She nodded toward Rio's freshly painted hoofs.

"Quite the dandy, isn't he? I thought his new owner——"

"New owner?" The car keys fell to the dirt. "You've sold Rio? Without asking me if——"

"I didn't sell him." Greg's calm words cut across her accusation. "He's a present for a pretty lady."

Stacy's world went black. Pretty lady. Greg was giving Rio to Lucy Fraser. A woman who probably didn't even know one end of the horse from another. "I hate you, Gregory Ferris," she said in a low, fierce voice. "You have no right."

Greg frowned across Rio's back. "Listen, Slim——"

"No, you listen. I'm the one who sat up nights with that horse. I'm the one who sided with you when C.B. said he couldn't be saved. Damn you." Hot tears sprang in her eyes. "I'm the one who named him Rio because he was red and Colorado means red and I said he'd run fast like a river and you agreed and I'll never forgive you for this."

Greg grabbed her as she stooped to gather the keys from the dust. "Where are you going?"

"Home."

"Not in my car." He gave a rueful laugh at the look of shock on her face. "Your mom accidentally let the cat out of the bag."

Too hurt and angry about Greg's treachery to even consider her mother's betrayal, Stacy threw the car keys at Greg. They connected with his chest. "Here are the damned keys. I bought the car with your money, anyway. Not because I give one damn about you, but because I didn't want anything of yours around to remind me of you. Not even your stupid money." She shook loose of his grasp. "I don't need a ride. I'll walk."

She took three steps. There was a rush of air and then a thick rope settled around her shoulders. Before Stacy could react, the loop tightened and she was pulled backward, her arms pinned to her sides. "Gregory Ferris, you release me this instant!" Greg pulled on the rope, hand over hand, hauling Stacy over to the corral where he stood. Leaning back, she dug in her heels. Her efforts were wasted. Greg reeled her in as easily as if she were an undersize trout. "I demand you untie me." Her fists clenched at her sides, she tossed back her hair and glared at him. "I don't know what you think you're doing, Gregory Ferris, but you're going to be very sorry," she promised.

"That remains to be seen, doesn't it?" Greg said calmly, lashing her to an upright corral pole. He pulled a clean handkerchief from his pocket and gagged her with it. Stacy gargled furiously. Greg's eyes crinkled against the sun and his mouth slowly broadened into a wide grin. "I should have done that years ago." He shoved his hat back on his head. "Now I want you to listen and listen good, Mrs. Ferris. In the first place, you ought to know damned good and well I wouldn't give Rio to anyone but you." He ignored the garbled sounds coming from Stacy. "The fact that you don't is almost enough to convince me that I ought to point you in the direction of Colorado Springs and give you a swift kick

in the pants to start you on your way." He stepped back
with a laugh as Stacy lashed out at him with her foot.
"That's not the only time you've been dead wrong lately.
I didn't tell you about C.B.'s will because I didn't want
you thinking exactly what you thought—that the only
reason I wanted you was because the rest of my ranch
came with you."

She managed to spit out the gag. "You didn't want
me at all."

He gave her an exasperated look. "Damn it, Slim, I
told you when you were ten I'd marry you. When did I
ever tell you I changed my mind?"

"The day we got married. You said if you hadn't been
such a jackass and I hadn't been such a damned idiot,
we never would have gotten married."

"And I meant it. Not married then. Not that way.
Dammit, Slim, did you think I'd forgotten your plans?
The white dress, the church, our friends, your dad giving
you away? I cost you all that because I couldn't keep
my pants on. I would have kicked myself black and blue
if that would have set things right again for you. In the
end, I gave C.B. the promise he asked for."

"Promise?"

"That I'd wait until you grew up."

"C.B.? He knew?" Her thoughts were so chaotic it
was a wonder she could speak.

"He knew something was wrong and I could never lie
to him," Greg said simply. "C.B. convinced me that you
were too young to be married. He asked me to keep my
distance from you, to give you an opportunity to experience life outside the Valley. Letting you return to
college was hard enough, but when you took the job at
the bank in Colorado Springs I damned near broke my
promise to C.B. Only by then he was so ill and there

wasn't a damned thing I could do for him. Except keep my promise to him. It seemed like such a little thing. A little thing that was a hell of a lot tougher that I expected,'' he added roughly.

"C.B. made you promise not to see me?'' Stacy was so stunned she was having trouble absorbing Greg's words.

"Why do you think he always let you know in advance when I'd be out of town so you could come visit? C.B. knew being around you and not being able to claim you was too much to ask of any man.''

"Too much to ask of a man! I thought you hated me. You never even spoke to me for three years.'' The thought of three wasted years, three years filled with loneliness and pain, started a slow, burning anger.

Greg gave her a lopsided smile. "When you were ten, marrying you seemed like a practical idea. You knew horses and you came with a ranch. By the time you were eighteen, you were stirring my hormones with a vengeance. I didn't care if you hated horses and came with nothing more than the clothes on your back, I just knew you had to belong to me.'' He hesitated. "I didn't try very hard that night to argue you out of the notion of sleeping together because I wanted you so badly. I still do.''

"You want me,'' Stacy repeated through clenched teeth. "What about Lucy Fraser?''

"Lucy and I share a common goal in helping Toby. Nothing more. I've never slept with her. I made a promise to C.B. and I kept it. I also made a promise to you on our wedding day and I've kept that. There's been no woman since our marriage. I know I let you think there was more between Lucy and me...'' He paused, smiling warmly at her. "I love you, you know. I can't remember when I haven't. When your mom said you'd be here for Mary Beth's wedding, I decided it was time to tell you to get your sweet behind back here where you belong.''

"Only I beat you to the punch by asking for a divorce.'' She was barely controlling her voice, much less her temper.

"You could have knocked me over with a feather.'' Greg unwrapped the coils of rope and released her.

"I'd prefer to knock you over with a telephone pole,'' Stacy said, incensed. She grabbed the lariat from him. Her loop was as swift and accurate as his. Fortunately Greg was leaning against a pole, so she didn't have to drag him. A couple of swift, tight turns and Greg was bound to the corral. The other end of the rope was quickly fastened to Rio's saddle horn. A quiet word to the well-trained sorrel and he backed up, keeping the rope taut.

Greg opened his mouth to countermand her order and then closed it. Stacy had counted on his unwillingness to confuse the horse. Standing beside Rio, her hand on his saddle, Stacy glared furiously at Greg. "Why didn't you ask me what I wanted to do? You had no right to make my decisions for me. You had no right to decide that I had to go to college and had to work somewhere else. You had no right to decide I was too young and immature to make my own decisions. No sane woman would stay married to an arrogant, chauvinistic thug like you. How dare you believe you had the right to tell me to get my sweet behind... ?'' She gnashed her teeth at the words. "Sweet behind. Of all the patronizing, smug, pompous jackasses!'' She was hollering at the top of her lungs but she didn't care who heard her. "Any woman with a lick of sense would run from you just as far and as fast as she could.''

"Damn it, Slim, didn't you hear me say I love you?"

A quiver of rage shook her entire body. "You love me. You love me!" she shrieked. "You have a pretty funny way of showing it—divorcing me."

Rio snorted and nervously pawed the ground.

"You're the one who insisted on a divorce. All I was trying to do was buy time until I figured out what was going on."

"So you came snooping around in Colorado Springs."

"I had to know if there was another man in your life."

"When you found out there wasn't, you still planned to divorce me." The right response would convince her.

"I couldn't tell you I loved you with that damned will of C.B.'s hanging over my head. That's why I had to have the ranch back. I thought after we got divorced I could tell you I loved you and you'd know I meant it because the only thing I could possibly want from you then was you. Hell, Slim, I didn't want to tell you about the will and have you feel obliged to stay married to me. I thought you should have a choice."

"A choice? I haven't had a choice in anything that's happened since we slept together three years ago." The thought of the needless suffering she and Greg had both endured, the enforced separation—all lent fuel to the conflagration. If Gregory Ferris thought she was going to quietly accept his outrageous manipulation of her life, no matter how well-meaning... "Damn you, Greg, who the hell appointed you God?" Whirling, Stacy dashed across the yard.

It wouldn't take Greg long to get loose and put Rio up, but she didn't need long. She turned the corner of the ranch house. The front door was out of Greg's sight. Quietly she went in, easing the door shut behind her. She quickly found what she wanted. The blinds in Greg's bedroom were half open and she peeked outside. Greg was already free and unsaddling Rio. She moved faster. His bed was too long. She dashed into the pink bedroom and gathered all the pillows. Taking them to Greg's room, she stacked them along with Greg's, making a tottering temporary headboard. Greg came into the house hollering her name. Taking a deep breath, Stacy started unbuttoning her blouse. She understood how Greg's promise had bound him, but this was one decision she intended to make on her own.

"Slim? Where the hell are you? I know you're still here."

She lay down gingerly on the bed, mentally crossing her fingers that the springs wouldn't betray her.

Greg's footsteps clattered up the stairs. One by one he opened the doors to the upstairs rooms, calling her name. The last door he came to was to his own bedroom. "Slim?"

Stacy swallowed hard. Her arms folded behind her head, a hopefully serene smile on her face, she peered at Greg from under the brim of C.B.'s old Stetson pulled low over her face. Greg froze inches from the old battered boots propped nonchalantly on the footboard of his bed. His gray eyes turned smoky opaque.

Heat cascaded through Stacy's body. Struggling to appear at ease, she pulled the grass stalk she was chewing from her mouth. "I'm staying, but with a few conditions. No more making my decisions for me."

"You can make your own decisions." Greg tossed his hat.

Stacy's stomach gave an excited little quiver as the hat landed on a bed post. "Equal partners or nothing."

"Equal partners." He unbuttoned the cuffs of his denim work shirt.

"I get to paint the whole house pink."

Greg sat down on the edge of the bed and tugged off a boot. "The hell you do." He tossed the second boot to the floor and stood up. He paused with his hand on his belt buckle. Picking up the phone near the bed, he dialed, never taking his eyes from her. "Dan. I'm going to be tied up the rest of the day. Take care of the chores for me. I'll be at the ranch house if any emergency comes up, but it damned well better be a gigantic emergency if you bother me."

Squawking noises came from the receiver. Greg's gaze roved over Stacy, his eyes dark with male desire. She felt the blood rushing through her veins. Her body must be as rosy as the Sangre de Cristos at sunset.

"Yeah, that was Slim who drove in," Greg said. "Yeah, she's going to stay this time." He laughed into the phone. "No, she's not wearing those sissy city clothes." He dropped the receiver back in the cradle and reaching down, trailed his hard, callused fingers between her breasts and down her trembling stomach. "I wonder what Dan would have said if I'd told him you were lying here wearing nothing more than C.B.'s old Stetson and a pair of beat-up boots."

"He'd probably wonder why you were just standing there jawing," Stacy said tartly.

Greg grinned. A second later his jeans hit the floor.

Let

HARLEQUIN ROMANCE®

take you

BACK TO THE **RANCH**

Come to the Rocking J Ranch, not too far from
Cactus Gulch, Arizona.

Meet sexy J. D. Vaughn—once a rodeo cowboy, now a *very*
successful rancher who's giving the other ranchers a run for their
money. *And meet* Deanna Leighton, the only vet in Cactus
Gulch...and the only woman who's giving J.D. a hard time!

Read ON THE LINE, an exciting new Romance from
Anne Marie Duquette—who truly makes love an adventure!

Available in November wherever Harlequin Books are sold.

HARLEQUIN ROMANCE®

A Halloween treat that's better than candy and almost as good as a kiss!

Two delightful frightful Romances from two of our most popular authors:

HAUNTED SPOUSE by Heather Allison
(Harlequin Romance 3284)
"Frizzy Lizzie" the Scream Queen confronts her handsome ex-husband—over a haunted house!

TO CATCH A GHOST by Day Leclaire
(Harlequin Romance 3285)
Zach Kingston wants to debunk Rachel Avery's family ghost. Rachel objects—and so does the ghost!

Available in October—just in time for Halloween!—wherever Harlequin books are sold.

Harlequin Romance invites you...

BACK TO THE

As you enjoy your Harlequin Romance® BACK TO THE RANCH stories each month, you can collect four proofs of purchase to redeem for an attractive gold-toned charm bracelet complete with five Western-themed charms. The bracelet will make a unique addition to your jewelry collection or a distinctive gift for that special someone.

One proof of purchase can be found in the back pages of each BACK TO THE RANCH title...one every month until May 1994.

To receive your gift, please fill out the information below and mail four (4) original proof-of-purchase coupons from any Harlequin Romance **BACK TO THE RANCH** title plus $2.50 for postage and handling (check or money order—do not send cash), payable to Harlequin Books, to: **IN THE U.S.**: P.O. Box 9057, Buffalo, NY, 14269-9057; **IN CANADA**: P.O. Box 622, Fort Erie, Ontario, L2A 5X3.

Requests must be received by June 30, 1994.

Please allow 4-6 weeks after receipt of order for delivery.

BACK TO THE RANCH

NAME: _____

ADDRESS: _____

_____

CITY: _____

STATE/PROVINCE: _____

ZIP/POSTAL CODE: _____

ONE PROOF OF PURCHASE   089 KAX